M.Y. Diallo was born on May 10, 1993, in Conakry, Guinea, where he studied experimental science in high school in order to attend medical school. After two years of medical school, he came to the USA to continue his studies, and that is where he fell in love with writing.

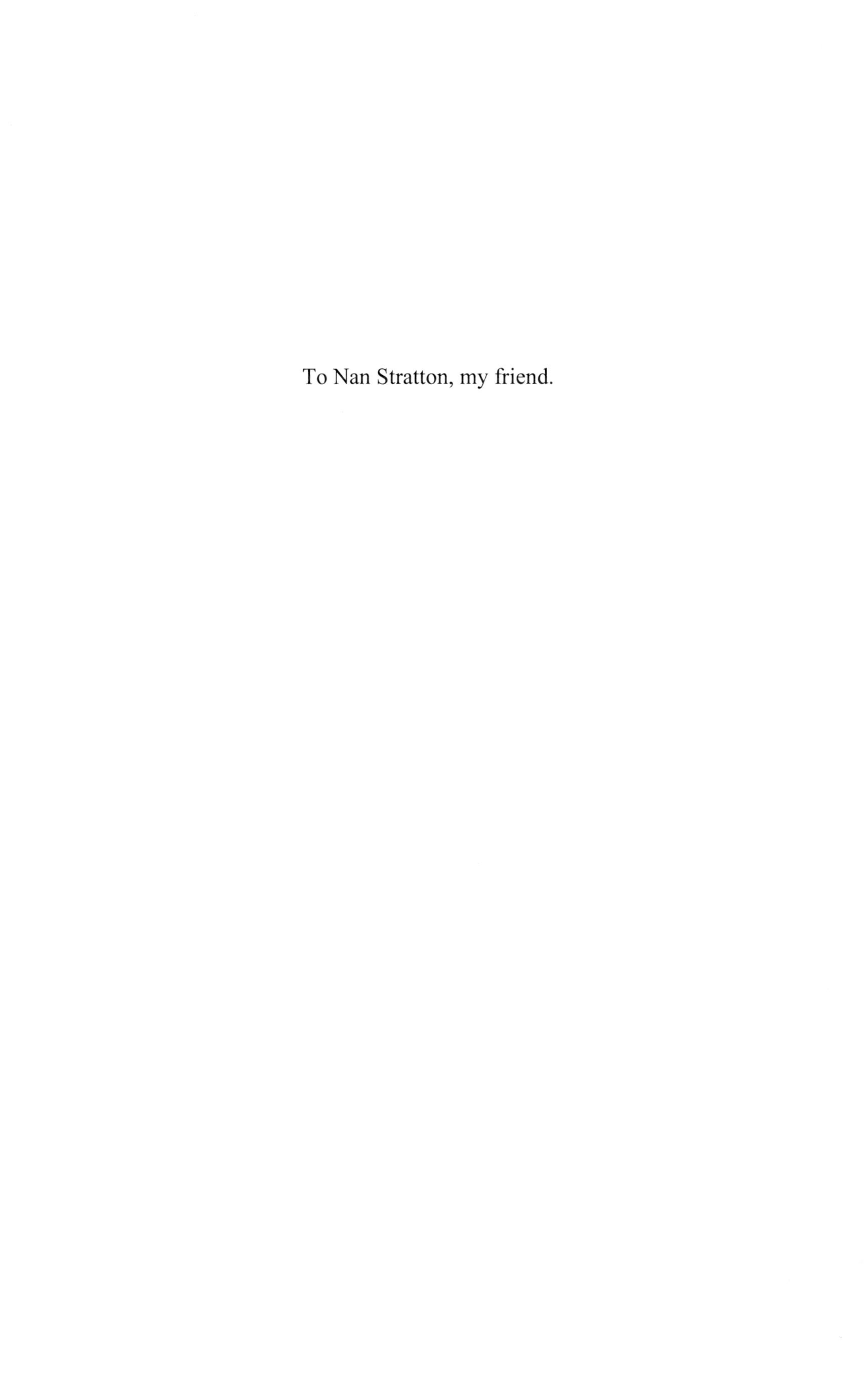

To Nan Stratton, my friend.

M.Y. Diallo

The Invisible Neighborhood

Austin Macauley Publishers™
London • Cambridge • New York • Sharjah

Ordering Information:
Quantity sales: special discounts are available on quantity purchases by corporations, associations, and others. For details, contact the publisher at the address below.

Publisher's Cataloguing-in-Publication data
Diallo, M.Y.
The Invisible Neighborhood

ISBN 9781641829236 (Paperback)
ISBN 9781641829243 (Hardback)
ISBN 9781645366423 (ePub e-book)

Library of Congress Control Number: 2020904750

www.austinmacauley.com/us

First Published (2020)
Austin Macauley Publishers LLC
40 Wall Street, 28th Floor
New York, NY 10005
USA

mail-usa@austinmacauley.com
+1 (646) 5125767

Chapter 1

The Lonely Boy

Irresponsible, selfish, tyrants, and inferior of all the creatures made by the creator are what they think of mankind. They always wake up, hoping a different view of the world positively but end up disappointed. Every generation of human brought to life, on planet Earth, was a deception for them, but they didn't care until they felt threatened by Mother Nature because of humans' foolishness. They had to make it stop. Otherwise, there won't be home for their descendants. When scientists warned humans about them, no one wanted to believe. Mankind never listens, humans have always thought that they are the only superior kind in the universe. Even after being shown proof by experts that there are other creatures living somewhere, humans still don't believe. Being stubborn as a mule, humans always need evidence; it's better to stay away from some evidences. The scariest and most shocking thing is that even scientists didn't know those creatures are among humans. We don't know that our daily life is shared with different kind of species.

***

Twenty-three years ago, two computer-programing engineers, Mr. Charles Layoun and Mrs. Olivia Layoun, started their jobs at the NASA. The couple met in college. Sharing the same ambitions and values, which was science, they became closer and fell unbelievably in love. They were the genius couple of their generation in their field. The two scientists were giving conferences at the prestigious University of Harvard. Here, they caught the attention of the NASA's director, who needed young, ambitious, and determined recruits to put the world in a better place.

A year after being recruited, they found out that there is no way out from the strong love they had for each other back in college, so they decided to spend the rest of their lives together. The beauty of their love was exceptional; it was the groovy kind of love.

The couple became important for the agency. Devoted to their job, they almost did not have a social life except for their newly born child. They preferred staying late at work more than going to a cocktail party with important people in suits, who they considered lazy people. Late one night, Mr. Layoun and his wife were about to leave the office when they made an incredible discovery. They prevented its realization temporarily, but they knew it will happen in the future—it was just a matter of time. It has to be stopped before it is too late. Frightened to death, they went to see the authorities with concrete explanations, but unfortunately, enticed by greed and power, the authorities' agents were determined to use all in their power to stop the couple from disclosing any information, and use this opportunity for their own agenda. The couple did not have any choice but to withdraw from the world of science because they felt threatened by their discovery. They were trapped between two hostile worlds. Before getting on their way, running for their survival, and their son's safety, they entrusted him and some documents that would be given to him when he reached the age of maturity.

Abandoning him was not an easy thing to do, but it was something necessary. Luckily, they had long-standing friends of trust, Mr. Benyamin Barry, and his wife, Mrs. Samira Barry, a loyal and respected family, living a peaceful life. Mr. Barry was the teammate of James' father until he retired.

For any young child, Mr. and Mrs. Barry are the last family to choose to spend the rest of their life with: a family that has never had the chance to know how to raise a child, the situation presented the potential for problems. For James's parents; however, it was the right family. It is an extraordinary couple, living an ordinary life far from the prying eyes in the countryside, and they can teach him all about his parents when the time comes. Mr. and Mrs. Layoun standing at the door, remembering the happiness and joy he brought into their lives the day he was born, it was hard for them, abandoning him, knowing that it is going to be a long goodbye or even worse, a forever goodbye.

Time to leave, but Mr. Layoun tries so hard to untie his wife's arms around the tiny child, she did not want to let go. They step out shedding tears, waving their hands, and saying goodbye to James, who was only three years old.

At his young age, James used to be haunted by a dream that he could not understand because of its darkness.

James is now seventeen years old. He has grown to become a lanky mild natured man with his arms as broomsticks, an unusually large head and grasshopper-thighs, his face is covered with acne. Bespectacled, most often when he is stuck in front of his computer. You can recognize him by his old, big, black leather jacket that has contact with water only once a month; this explains his unpopularity in school. James is extremely shy. He will never look at you in the eye, especially if you are a girl. It is his last year of high school. Life in high school is hell for kids like James. It's a jungle where only the law of the strongest prevails. One more year, and he will finally be getting rid of his nightmare.

James is not aware that he is not living with his biological parents. It is time for him to learn who his real parents are, but the couple has some difficulties tackling the issue. One morning, without checking whether James was still in bed or not, Samira asks her husband if he has made up his mind about telling James the truth, because she is not ready yet. He is their only son and they are all attached to him. James hears noises in the living room, and he rises up from his bed. At the moment, Benyamin wants to open his mouth to answer, he sees James coming from his room and interrupting them.

"What are you guys talking about?" asks James indifferently.

Samira lowers her head and says nothing, James has no clue what they are talking about, but he has a feeling that is it important considering the sadness on their faces. After a long moment of silence in the room looking at the helpless couple staring at each other, he begins to worry without knowing what is going on. What is he going to hear? Soon, Samira opens her mouth to talk, but James interrupts her and says, "You will tell me whenever you are ready, and whatever it is I'll understand."

In his turn, the father cuts off the words of poor James, whispering, "My son, you are adopted."

A monumental dead silence invades the living room; James cannot find the exact word to express himself. "Wow!" he finally mutters.

Samira starts crying and storms out of the living room and enters her room while Benyamin tries fighting back his tears. He follows his wife in the room, but she continues crying, repeating, "He hates us, doesn't he?" several times.

James goes into the room, finds Samira wiping her tears from her cheeks. Trying to hide her pain, she keeps her red eyes open and smiles at him, "I'm fine honey," she mumbled. James slips slowly between them, and confesses to them that the fact he has been adopted does not change the love that he has for them, and anyway, he is still stuck on them because the love that he has for them is incomparable to anything else; they are his family, they have always been there for him, they taught him everything.

"But why now, why didn't you tell me all this time?" James asked.

"You weren't supposed to know. At least not now, I made a promise to your parents." Answers Benyamin

"What! My birth parents told you to inform me that you adopted me? It doesn't make any sense," James snapped.

"It does not make sense if it's an adoption."

James is lost, trying to figure out what they are talking about. "OK! Let me simplify: your father and I were best friends. I was his mentor and then his colleague until I retired," said Mr. Barry

"And?" he asked confusedly

"And what?"

"How does this explain my adoption?"

"It doesn't yet, but when we get to the right time you will have the explanation you need. In the meantime I can give you a briefcase that your parents left for you before you said goodbye to them. It contains documents that will help you know something about them."

Barry goes into his room and opens another door that leads to a secret underground, that only he and his wife know about. It is a place containing computers and files that he had received from James' father at their last meeting. He opens a safe and takes out a briefcase, removes a few documents and places them in the trunk, and then closes it. He goes and finds James sitting in the living room, confused, thinking that he is left by his parent because he is a terrible child. Mr. Barry gives him the documents, to allow him to find out a little about his birth parents.

James flips through the file, realizes that he has a lot in common with his parent. He discovers that they were the youngest students recruited to work for the NASA, but he does not find any trace that shows the cause of their disappearance from his life. He asks Barry if the files are complete. Barry answers confidently, "Yes, why?"

Knowing that James is too intelligent to believe that the files are complete, Mr. Barry already has a plan to make him believe they are. James must not know the secret hidden in these documents; otherwise he risks drawing attention and putting himself in danger. Barry shows him his personal files of the time spent with Mr. Layoun till his retirement. James finds maximum conformity. After finishing browsing the files, he hands them over to Barry, who tells him never to talk about it to anyone, not even his best friend if he has any. His life depends on it.

James leaves the house to clear up his mind, but he does not arrive to erase from his memory the tumultuous events of the morning. For days he is intrigued by the fact that at the age of three years old his family abandoned him for a reason that he is not yet allowed to know. Whenever he starts asking questions about his biological parents, his adoptive parents avoid the subject by telling him to wait until the day comes. A day will come when he will not need to ask them to find out. James begins to understand why his pathetic life is largely shrouded in mystery. He realizes that it is not a coincidence that his life has always been based in the countryside, where he cannot make many friends, although, he is not disconnected from the world of technology. He has an incomparable brain that can easily be detected by a rather undesirable group of people, which is why he must keep a low profile as his parents have urged him to adopt. He should never do anything that will make him stand out to people.

Class starts in two days. James must be registered for his last year of high school, so he goes there without wasting any further time. In the countryside, school places are always limited. When he arrives at school, nobody pays attention to him. Being used to being ignored by his peers, he does not feel uncomfortable about it anymore as before when he was ridden by feelings of inferiority. James steps directly into the principal's office. The lack of communicating with strangers makes James respectable, he intimidates older people with his quietness while having nightmare with people of his generation. James listens more than he talks, and that is what makes him mysterious.

"Come in James!" the principal said. He takes a seat after passing along greetings from his parents to the director. Sabrina Smith is the director; she is a wonderful woman who has been in charge of the community high school since last year. James caught her attention when she first came. She likes James because of his politeness and good behavior towards everybody in school, and she knows James's parents well. After a long discussion with the director about his project of study for this year, he signs in and leaves the office. Once outside the office, he fatuously jostles Sofi without realizing it, and she falls down with her books and a stack of papers scattering all around. He spontaneously gets down to help. She raises her head. He is mesmerized by the fall of her long dark lashes over her deep blue eyes. For the first time in his life, he extends a hand to the girl. After having helped her to get up, he notices that her face is not familiar to him. Sofi smiles lowers her head and tucks her hair behind her ear. Nervous, he cannot express himself, but part of his mind wants to make her acquaintance before the other students infect her with the virus of the hatred.

Sofi is a beautiful smart, ambitious and charismatic girl filled with a rather twisted sense of humor when she tries to be funny.

James begins to apologize stutteringly, and asks her name. She squeezes her eyes shut and open them. "Seriously!!! You just knocked me down and the first thing that comes to your mind is to flirt with me?"

James apologizes a second time, "No, no absolutely not. I wanted to make sure you're OK—I thought it was the least I could do after accidentally knocking you down."

She accepts his excuses and turns around without telling him her name, but James insists in knowing her name, and also proposes to be her guide. She smiles and James continues wagging around her. James asks her what her favorite subjects are; knowing that is the key to his relationship with her. There is no doubt for him, if she likes literary matters his chances of being her friend are little, but if she prefers exact matters such as math, he will probably be her friend. When he finishes asking the question, he holds his breath because of being afraid of the answer that he will receive. Fortunately, she is a nerd just like him. He exhales deeply, with relief. "What is it?" she asks.

"No, nothing. I couldn't breathe, but I'm good now. I regained control of my lungs," he replies.

She did not know that she had the control of poor James's lungs.

Eyes wide-open James asks with seriousness, "What did you say? You like math and physics!"

"Yes," the girl answers with a surprisingly.

"Me too," James says with an excited voice.

She tells him that she has come to finish her last year of high school, and she has been living with her mother again for the last two months.

In the middle of their conversation Georgina Kura arrives and interrupts them. She is a wicked witch and the queen of the school. Georgina and her two minions, Alicia and Rose can make anybody's life look like hell, you have no choice if you are targeted. They start spitting their venom at him. "Oh isn't that sweet, girls? Finally, poor James has a friend with whom to look after his loneliness," she says with facetiousness.

James is embarrassed and humiliated by Georgina once again. Enraged, James leaves the new girl speechless; she could not help to notice the huffiness on his face. James is being punished for declaring his feelings to the wrong person. He has been pining over Georgina since elementary school, and has never dared to tell her because he knows she does not have the same feelings. He is a geek who has no friends and he is sentimentally unavailable, he has no strength attach with no one. James only thinks about studies. One day, after being convinced by Jackson, he decides to drop off his heavy burden telling her how he felt, unfortunately he was spurned. Since that day, James had a gigantic hole in his heart because of her. Sofi glances longingly at Georgina and her upper lip curls in disgust. Then she hugs her books and moves along without saying a word.

She enters the office, "Hello mother!" she says enthusiastically. The principal smiles, "Hi! Honey," says Sabrina then she walks behind her desk to hug her daughter. Sofi takes a seat and starts explaining her little adventure with one of the students to her mother, from the beginning, until the point at which Georgina interrupted them. Sabrina forbids her from being Georgina's friend because despite her the most popular girl in school she the perfect definition of selfish. She does not care about anyone; she does whatever she wants, even if it is something that can hurt her friends. The girl reminds her mother that she received a good education and she is not there to make friends. But she does not forget to ask her mother about James: who is he, and how long has he been at that school?

The mother pretends not to be happy to see her daughter being interested in James, although she is relieved it is not one of those dimwits wandering in the corridor with their big muscles and tiny brains always carrying and football equipment; she has known the lonely boy for a year and she has never heard of him committing acts of vandalism as the others do. He is one of the good students and the perfect boy for her daughter.

James explains to his parents that he met a girl at school. She is new, and she is nice, and all that he knows about her is that she lives with her mother. James' parents suggest him to be careful of where he sets his foot if he wants her to be his friend or more, he must know her first. He does not have any other choice but to abide by the family rule which is not trusting anyone. He goes back to his room. James has the privilege of inheriting not only the characteristic of two geniuses but also the technology that helps him explore his potential. James learned programming at the age of ten, so hacking into a server of any kind is easy for him.

While typing on the keyboard, his brain starts recollecting the data from the morning event at school with the mysterious girl. Soon, his brain is invaded by her angelic smile. He stops typing and start thinking about how to get back to a civilized conversation with her without any awkwardness. Then a desperate but brilliant idea pops out, but first he needs to do some research on her before letting her into his life which is an easy task for him, since he has a software program that allows him to recognize any person registered in any database of any institution. All he needs is to know her name and the name of her family, so he sleeps on it.

After a long night stirred by a dream that will doubtlessly never happen with the girl, James wakes up happy, with a delightful smile on his face that his parents had never seen before. The worried parents want to talk to James before he makes any mistake, but he is in rush, not wanting to be late on his first day of class. They decide to drop him off at school, so that they can have the opportunity to talk to him on the way. "Do you need a ride?" the father asked.

"Why?" he asked furrowing.

"Do we need a reason for that?"

"No, I guess, I'm just confused. What are you guys up to…?"

"Nothing, it's just that you can't be late the first day of class; come." Said Benyamin enthusiastically

"OK!" After a while in the car, sitting in an awkward silence James breaks the silence "What did I do? Go on, I know this ride is not free, but you do, have to be brief though. I can't afford having people see me with you. It's the first day of class. If you know what I mean!"

"No, we don't little ungrateful selfish brat." Said the dad. The parents look at each other and here it goes the lecture begins, but they hesitate a little; afraid to upset him as nowadays kids can be rebellious, and parents are not allowed to spank them from time to time. James glares at Benyamin with a challenging look, "I'm listening, because every time you come with me it's to get some information from me as if you were agents of the KGB, or CIA so I'm listening."

"OK! We've seen you happy today and we wanted to know if it's that girl."

"I don't know what you're talking about."

"Hum," said Benyamin gruffly.

"OK! Fine, maybe." James snapped

"What do you know about her?" Asked Samira

"Nothing, yet," he said nervously. "Then get to it." said Mr. Barry

"Yes, sir! Your wish is my command." James nodded.

"You know we love you, right?" The mother kisses him.

"Yes, and I love you too."

"Cool! Now get out!" said Benyamin

He pops out from the vehicle and Jackson calls out to him. When he arrives, Jackson asks if his parents are going to be dropping him off at school this year. "Nahhh, don't be a moron." He responded with uncertainty knowing that they might do it every day just to prevent him from making bad decisions.

Chapter 2

The Dream Girl

As soon as he gets in class, his eyes start darting around looking for the mysterious girl, but he does not see her. A few minutes later, the girl in his dreams arrives into the room with a gait out-of-the-ordinary, looking at her steps, while walking with gorgeous big eyes. She sees James sitting alone, who has his mouth and eyes wide open, staring at her until she arrives near him. "Can I sit here?" she smiled.

Lost in his imaginations James looks at behind him, then right and left he realizes that he is the one who she is talking to, "What?" he asks astonishingly.

"Can I sit here?" she repeats, pointing her finger to the sit next to James. James still cannot believe that she is talking to him; he is speechless. She smiles again and sits anyway, "Hi!" she says, "It's James, right?"

James whispers, "Finally, someone who remembers my name for the first time." She is not sure what she heard, so she asks what he has just whispered.

"Yes, yeah, totally yes, it's my name," he answers, "And you what's your name again?"

"Seriously, again! I told you that I'm not telling you my name."

"I've always been a curious person by nature, unless you want me to call you the mysterious girl."

"You call me that, and I'll kill you."

"Wow, slow down, you seem dangerous."

"You want me to show you my kill list?"

"No thanks, I am good, your name will be enough."

"Good luck with that."

"About what?"

"Knowing my name."

"You're weird, you know that?" James says.

"Yes, I hear that often."

James did not know that she had her reasons for not disclosing her name. This reason is that she does not want anyone to know that the headmistress is her mother, and at worst, to know whom her father is. She asks James about Georgina, what is deal between them. It is a sensible subject for James when it comes to Georgina, his pale face becomes red all of the sudden. He does not want to talk about it, but he also does not want to stop talking to her. "It's a long story." He confessed, but she lets him know that they have the time—the teacher is not there yet. James wants to make a deal with her. "Your name first. I know the name of everyone here," he said.

"Forget it," she snapped, but her curiosity does not let her give up, so she points to a girl in the class and asks him her name. "Rebecca." He said confidently

"No, I meant her last name. You just said that you know the name of everyone."

He turns his head and whispers to Rebecca's ear, "What's your last name?"

"Wow! I've been in the same class with you for three years and you don't know my name? Go away." Says Rebecca.

Given to his cleverness, the lonely boy asked Rebecca to tell him otherwise he'll tell her secret to everyone. Rebecca is so naïve: she does not know what James is talking about, but she does not want to take a risk, so she tells him her name. James does not know that the girl has heard everything. When he says the name, she smiles, "I heard you blackmail her. This explain your lack of friends." She said disdainfully.

"Please tell me your name. I'd really like to post a name on this beautiful smile."

The girl is motionless for a moment after realizing that he is really flirting. She locks eyes with him all of the sudden.

"I see you coming and this has to stop now." He smiles and she continues, "I'll tell you my name if you stop doing this thing with your smile. I don't like it, and I'm not interested."

"Don't worry; I'm not going to try anything. Anyway, I don't think I can survive another humiliation."

"Wow! Is it the fear of being rejected that keeps you from asking me out? That's interesting! Wait it's Georgi, isn't it?" she said mockingly

At the moment when he wants to answer, the teacher enters the class. Saved by the bell, he smiles. She insists as the teacher introduces himself, and the teacher interrupts them. "Hey, you two, am I interrupting something?"

"No sir," they both respond. The girl lowers her head.

"James, you already started to seduce the new girl, right?"

"Which one?"

"Sofi."

James lowers his head and looks at Sofi, smiles, "I got your name without your help," he mutters. The teacher asks James what he just whispered. "Nothing, just saying that if I didn't have your class, I would have abandoned school."

"Yeah, funny, now hold your tongue and listen."

Sofi is impressed by how he handled the situation. She does not stop staring at him until the end of class, and James tells her to stop ogling him with her irresistible look because he is not interested. She smiles and lowers hear head.

After the classes, James follows Sofi to talk to her and sees her enter the principal's office. To his surprise he hears Sofi say, "Mom." He looks through the windows and does not see anyone except the director. He listens to the conversation and he realizes that she is really the mother of Sofi. He waits for her to know that he saw her and heard everything, but it seems that she will stay there for a while.

This is a good start on his research. He now knows the name of Sofi from the teacher and knows where to start this research from the last name of the director. He rushes into his room and begins to search. He sees nothing important. He uses the name of the mother of Sofi, who is Sabrina Smith, and he still finds nothing relevant. However, he is relieved of being able to tell his parents that the girl is clean, but he remains wary. James and Sofi continue to see each other at school for a week, she notices that her guess about James not having friends besides her and Jackson was right, but everyone knows him because of his skills in everything at school. When the two are together, they feel a connection. James has still not told Sofi that he knows that the headmistress is her mother, so she would not know that he had spied on her. That could ruin their friendship, which is fragile at the moment.

One day after finishing class, James invites Sofi to have a drink and she agrees, giving him the time and the address where he can find her. He smiles, she looks at him blushing. "But just remember that it is not a date; it does not mean anything, OK?" she says to him.

"OK, OK!!!" James replies smirking.

"I'm serious" She added. James goes home happy. His mother is worried seeing James so happy, she has not seen him blooming like that for a long time or maybe never. She calls James' father in order to not be the only witness; otherwise James will deny it, and Mr. Benyamin won't believe it.

The father sits down and asks, "What is this beautiful smile, man I didn't know you can smile?"

"Today I think I have a date with Sofi."

"You think?"

"Yeah, she told me it does not mean anything, it's just a drink."

Samira's eyes go wide, "By drink you mean tea or something like ice-cream, right?"

"Of course!" he responded firmly

"OK! By the way, when are we going to see her?"

"Why do you want to see her? She is just a friend."

"That's why we want to see her. You never showed us a friend of yours except Jackson."

"Because I only have Jackson, duh; it sounds funny, but he's invisible like me; we are good together. That's what you've always wanted, isn't it? If we're done, I'd like to borrow your Jeep for this historic evening of mine."

"Are you sure she'll get into this pile of scrap metal, it's an antique car man, she won't."

"I have nothing else; she'll have to deal with it."

"OK! It's yours, just be careful."

"OK, thanks."

Excited, James arrives little bit early at Sofi's. She hears a car stop and looks through the window. She gets out quickly. James cannot stop stealing illicit peeks inside the house, but she shields his view by standing in front of him. "Are you alone?" He finally asked.

"Yep!"

"Don't you have anyone to introduce to me?" He simpered while shaking his head. "Nope! there is no one here that you need to know except me, now go open the door for me."

"Hum; OK." Without seeing anybody, he says, "Who is this woman I see? We would say our headmistress at school."

"We should go and get you some glasses, what do you think about that?"

"Why?" He asked confusedly

"Because it looks like to me that you see things upside down." Sofi sees the car and an awful image comes to her mind: a hearse, but she doesn't say anything. James tries to open the door, another Calvary for him: the door is blocked. After several attempts, he remains unable to open the door. He does not dare look Sofi in the eyes. She is behind him, staring at him and embarrassed for him. Sofi jumps and lands in the car. "Oh…look at you."

"Do like me," she says.

He replies, "I don't know how you did this. I don't want to know, and even if I knew it I would not try to commit suicide—I'm too young to die." Sofi smiles: she realizes how cute, funny and innocent he is. James manages to get into the car and they leave.

They arrive at the restaurant, place their orders and begin sincerely to discuss their extra-curricular activities. Sofi does nothing special in her spare time; she surfs on the Internet like any other teenager, chats with her friends from her old school, obsessed with music and rarely goes out of her room.

"I like having conversations with people that make me understand what the meaning of life is for them." She added while glaring at James

James is mesmerized by the depth of her emotions when she talks. Having nothing to do would be an understatement for James. He spends his days in his room, exploring new horizons in the world of computer programming, and sometimes he spends his time at the stadium with his best and only friend Jackson. Jackson has friends that James does not approve of, but at least they share the same love for soccer—well, he likes music too. "who's Jackson." She asked. "Jackson's my best friend you'll like him I promise."

Curious as always, James cannot retain himself from asking whom she lives in the big house with.

Sofi's heart starts pounding abnormally. "What?" She asked nervously. "You know at your house!" James retorted casually. All thoughts go through Sofi's mind: why is he interested in knowing who I live with, but she ends up answering, proving him right: it was the principal he claimed to have seen in the house. Without delay, James asks, as if surprised, "Why do you live with the director?"

"It's my mother, but I was not ready for the students to know that she's my mother. I apologize to have told you that you see things upside down. Anyway, is that myopia, or hypermetropia I don't know which one, do you know the difference?"

"No, I don't, and your secret is safe with me."

"What are you talking about?" she asks.

James didn't want to have any secrets from her because she wouldn't trust him if she ended up knowing that he knew it before. So he decides to tell her the truth. After having confessed to her, she accepted and she became proud of him since he told her the truth without any obligation. She said, "So you knew it all along?"

"Yes."

"OK, it's not going to last, but thank you." Sofi goes back on the subject of Georgina. It is a long and boring story that he doesn't want to explain in the restaurant especially for the sake of his happiest moment. He begs her not to ruin it, but once at home, he will tell her all she wants to know. She nods.

After a good time together, Sofi's curiosity does not let her enjoy the moment she glances at her phone. "I think it's my curfew." She said casually.

"Oh, already?"

"Yep, sorry!"

James gives her a ride home. When they arrive at Sofi's, she insists that he comes inside the house: she wants to introduce him to her mother. James is not sure if he is ready for the principal to know that he started philandering her daughter. He will not be able to bear the principal's disappointment if it comes to that. So he refuses, but for little he knows Sofi is a villain lurking behind an angel's face using her charm to get what she wants. "You won't make a beautiful girl like me beg you to come in my room, will you?"

James smiles. He knows that it is the first time that a girl has offered him something that is in his interest and not merely in the girl's; usually, when girls ask him something, it is about her homework.

Once inside, they find Sofi's mother in the living room. "You didn't tell me that we would have your friend over to visit—or I don't know how you say nowadays," the mother said.

"We just say friend, Mom, just friend. His name is James; he's cute, but a little awkward, clumsy and most of the time annoying."

"Clumsy? I know James is a nice guy, but I didn't know that he was clumsy."

"Oh! I think you don't know him well enough, the day we first met he upset me by knocking me off my feet with my books, I could've died you know?" She looks at James

"Sofi, stop talking, you're embarrassing me," whispered James.

"I thought you weren't ready for people to know I'm your mother."

"No worries, James knew it before I told him."

"Well, good to know. So how did your evening go?"

"Very well," they both answered at once.

"And why are you back so early if that's the case?"

"Nothing, we just wanted to come back," answered Sofi.

"OK! Does someone want some coffee?" asked Sabrina.

"Yes please," responded Sofi.

James said, "I think I've drunk enough for today."

"What…! What exactly did you drink? Alcohol?" she snaps at him.

"No, not at all, madam," James replied with panic.

"OK, fine. I'm going to bed," said her mother, adding, "If James wants to stay a little, you open the door and turn on the light."

"Mom…" Cried Sofi

"I'm just saying."

"OK. Good night, Mom. Go now, you're embarrassing me—we are just friends."

"I also think it is time for me to go home," says James.

"No, not until you tell me."

"What?"

"Your long story, that you couldn't tell me at the restaurant."

"Hoo nooo, I should have known. Please not that again."

"Do you want me to take my magic words out like when you refused to come in?"

"No, it's good. I'll tell you if you promise not to laugh."

"Promised and sworn."

"OK, if you want me to tell you the story you'll have to take a pen and a notebook you should write it. It is a true love story, maybe it will serve you someday." Sitting at the edge of her bed, she frowns.

"How a break-up love story could serve me someday? Stop being silly."

"OK! It's up to you."

Her curiosity is stronger than her; she is ready to do everything to know what happened.

"OK, OK, I'll write it, I'm taking a pen."

After some trouble in getting her backpack, she takes the pen and the notebook, and tells him to start. James is anxious, he does not like to talk about Georgina, but Sofi's obsession is becoming unbearable. She is not going to give up until he tells her.

"It was time for me to get out of my isolation last year," James starts, "so I decided to tell Georgina about my feelings for her. Are you writing this?" He asked.

"Yes, I'm getting it."

"Encouraged by Jackson, I went to find her after the soccer game organized by the high school. I confessed that I've been pining over her since the day I met her as she didn't know. She sent me strolling by offering me her little sister. Period. Did you get all that?"

"Oh, that's sad…" She looks at him, "Yes. Hold on, I'm on period."

"Are you writing period too? I meant end of the story, period sweetie."

"No, you didn't?"

"Ho…yes, I did."

"You're a dead man."

She starts running after him for a while. James looks at the time and realizes that it's late; he has to go before his parents get worried. Sofi escorts him to the door. "I've had a good time," she confesses.

"Me too." Smiles James. She hugs him. The lonely boy still does not believe that he spent a beautiful evening that he had never had before in his life. When Sofi steps back at the house, after an overwhelming feeling, she sees her mother in the kitchen looking for something to drink. "I couldn't sleep. It seems you had a good evening, didn't you?" she says.

"Yes, Mom, a good one that I hadn't had in a long time," Sofi says, lost in a deep thought. Sabrina waves her hand in front of her face.

"Do you like him?" Sabrina asks.

"What do you mean?" Sofi snapped as a guilty person would react. Sabrina glares at her challengingly. "Of course I like him, as a friend," she answers, and become silent for a moment lost in her thought again.

"OK..." Sabrina smiles, "I'm going back to my room because you're freaking me out right now."

After that evening which has marked James' life, he realizes that he has many things to learn. He does not delay to tell Jackson that he officially has a friend classified in the female specimen. and that she knows his history with Georgina, and he is a computer whiz, and she didn't care about any of these, she accepts him for who he is, with his bad jokes, and being emotionally damaged most of the time. Jackson finds it hard to believe; questioning his credibility about the story he told Sofi. "Are you sure that you told her the real history about you and Georgina? Not the one you invented?" Said Jackson.

"Whatever!" Responded James. Jackson is anxiously waiting to see this mysterious girl who has suddenly transformed the shy nerdy James into a jaunty jabberer. "I've already told her about you," James tells him to join him to the cafeteria during lunchtime to see her.

Chapter 3

Loyalty and Feelings

After being introduced to Sofi a week ago, Jackson starts having feelings for her, but dare not breathe a word about it to James. Today is the day when Jackson is unable to hide his feelings anymore, so he asks James about their relationship. There is nothing you can do when someone's desire gives away the loyalty; it is a shame, but only for the one who cares. Unfortunately Jackson is not one of them. He is the guy who would trade his grandma for one dance in a strip club. According to James he is a good guy though. It is not a surprise for James; he knows that Jackson is his best friend, but also someone who would not hesitate to betray his best friend for a girl. "Do not worry, Sofi and I are just friends," he replied, and he sees a joy on Jackson's face and asks him why this question.

"Do you mind if I make her mine?" asks Jackson.

"No, not at all, you have even my blessing," James answered with a frosty fake smile drawn on his face.

Happy, Jackson thanks him for his understanding and he start to work hard for it. He must impress her, which is not going to be easy. He goes to James for some tips about what kind of man she is interested in. The problem is that James does not really know what Sofi likes or dislikes. They are just friends, so there are limits not to cross. As long as these boundaries are not violated, James won't have anything to worry about. Days passé, Jackson, James, and Sofi spend good time together, but Jackson still has not asked Sofi out yet because she only sees James when they are together. Jackson feels invisible to her. He needs some help. Aware of the fact that James lacks of communication skills and a relevant social life, Jackson cannot argue that the ball is in the side of James this time. He might be useful to Jackson for once. When Jackson solicits James for help, the lonely boy does not want to jeopardize his friendship with Sofi, he tries to avoid the subject with flimsy excuses.

Being always bothered by his friend, who does not have the word giving up in his dictionary, James decides to listen to Jackson.

"I thought you were the best with girls," James says.

"Yes, but I do not understand her, she is different, everyone at school tries to flirt with her, but nobody dares talking to her. It's like you are the only one who does not see her as everyone sees her."

"Why would they be frightened by her? I think she's great," James asks surprisingly.

"Of course she's great; since she's here you feel good, she made you even forget about Georgina."

"No, she didn't! I forgot Georgina the day she made me regret to have had liked her."

"What? But you have little feelings for her, is not it?"

James stare at Jackson, refuses to admit it.

"It never crosses your mind that she can be your girlfriend and not just your friend?"

"I had never thought about it, and she advised me not to even think about it. Now, I would like you to do me a favor by stopping your stupid questions."

"OK! Since you were the one advised, and not I, I will try my luck tomorrow."

The next day, Jackson sees Sofi at the aisle of the school. He sucks in a deep breath and walks over to her. Then he impulsively asks her out for a movie the same evening. Surprised, eyes wide open like someone who just saw a ghost, Sofi's heart throbs she swallows heavily as she looks into his eyes, "I, I...have plans, maybe another time?" Stammered Sofi. After a moment of standing in an awkward silence Jackson shuffles back to his corner. Jackson is certain of the unsuccessfulness of his plan, but he is not worried since she has postponed and not rejected his offer. On his way to go share the big news with James, Jackson cannot help to have multiple thoughts running through his mind. Thoughts that he is trying so hard to shake out of his mind but can't. thoughts some of which are encouraging him to stop lying to himself and admit that she is just not interested in him. At his arrival he stands in front of James debating about what to tell him. James did not need to hear from him to know that things did not go as the charming boy would have expected.

"Before you went there, I warned you, didn't I? welcome to the club my friend," retorted James

"What?"

"Are you out of your mind or you are pretending to forget?"

"No, yes, no, please bro you've got to talk to her," he said nervously.

"No!"

"Please. It's all I need."

"That's what you said last time."

"This time I promise."

"OK. We'll see."

Several days pass and James' intervention has not been successful as he would have hoped "Are you sure this girl is into boys?" Jackson asked, "Why?" James frowned.

"Because I did all I can to impress her but it looks like she does not see me."

Smirking, James gives him a stern look "No, man! You cannot impress her like that, she is different, you have to be yourself."

"What kind of girl is not interested in something in this twenty first century world, I think she's a homosexual, and if you tell me the opposite I'll kill you," snapped Jackson.

"OK! I won't say anything."

"I'm done with her."

Very angry, Jackson leaves. James calls Sofi, and asks her what happened between her and Jackson because he had just left his house with anger as if he had something to reproach himself with. "Why are you call me for this kind of rubbish. Ho…I see it's because you send him to me after I explicitly told you that I'm not interested."

"He was doing all this for you?"

"Yes, I'm not a kid, and he's not my type."

"OK. What's your type?"

Sofi hangs up and puts the phone down. James' is flabbergasted by her action, but for the sake of their friendship he refrains from calling back.

After all that is forgotten, they decide to be good friends for the rest of the long semester. The results of the midterm are posted, James notices something strange when he looks at the list he sees several names that are familiar to him and sees another name that is half-familiar to him, the name of Sofi. Looking at the list, James sees the name Sofi Parker, unless it's the name of another, but he is sure and certain that is the same Sofi. He waits for her at the aisle until her arrival to know how the results of the midterm were for her. Without knowing what is going on, she is thrilled about her grades in all subjects. When she asks him, he also answers to her with an unusual tone. She feels disappointment in his tone.

"What's the matter?" she asks.

"What's your name?" asked James

Astonished, Sofi cannot find the right words to reply.

"You will tell me the truth, right?" James asks again.

"Yes, but I'm not ready yet."

"OK. Whenever you're ready."

"Thank you for your understanding."

During the evening at home, Sofi is pondering about what happened at school. Realizing that Sofi is plunged into deep thought for a while, Sabrina gets worried, but she cannot do anything because Sofi can be a stubborn girl sometimes. When she sticks her mind to something, she doesn't change her mind.

James knows that it will be wrong of him to judge Sofi that she has lied to him about her parents, he did not insist for an immediate answer, but he is hurt. He scurries into his room to restart his search on his mysterious friend again. He searches for a long time and finds several Parkers but cannot connect any of them to Sofi. His worries start growing exponentially.

After having spent a night shrouded with horrible thoughts, James is debating whether he should give her the benefit of the doubt or not. Sofi notices his change in demeanor. She sees him from a distance in the cafeteria and continues nervously fiddling her thumbs, staring at him and second-guessing herself about joining him. She cannot turn to Jackson because he is one of her broken-hearted victims. James has always been taught to stay away from what he does not understand, and Sofi is one of those cases, so he rises up from his chair and leaves before being enticed by temptation of joining her. Sofi knows what she has done to make James upset, and the only thing she can do to make up for this misunderstanding is to tell him what he wants to know. She needs a best laid plan that will not go awry, for the sake of her friendship with James. She heads toward James, he gets up and leaves the cafeteria. James did not tell his parents about Sofi because of fear of what their reaction might be since they had warned him. The principal summons James in her office, "Hello James, take a seat." She waves her hand. James pulls up the chair and tentatively sits. "The reason why I call you in is because of Sofi. She seems off these days, and I was wondering if you have an idea about what is bothering her?" She continued.

"No ma'am," he mumbled, but Sabrina insists. For the first time James is annoyed by one if his favorite person.

"She's not my girlfriend, you know?" He retorts

"Yes, I know, but you're her friend, I mean her only friend, and if something goes wrong, I thought I could always ask you or count on you, right?"

"Yes, I know, well it's about her name I thought your name is Sabrina Smith and why Sofi's name is Parker?"

In the middle of their conversation James lets out a dorky high-pitched laugh. Sabrina squints she cannot help to smile. James shuts his mouth in embarrassment. He is flattered that Sofi is troubled because of him.

"Oh! Is it because of that?" she says surprisingly.

"Yes, this is important to me; I prefer a trustworthy friend over a friend hiding her identity."

Sabrina starts explaining lies with no pang of conscience, "Her father is called Parker and after my divorce, I took over my maiden name." She said emotionally.

"OK, but you didn't have to tell me!"

"I know, and I did it for my little girl. She is everything to me."

"Oh! I'm sorry for causing this pain ma'am." Said James.

James picks up his phone and calls Sofi who rushes to take the phone after she had left several messages to James who had not replied. She picks up the phone, "What's wrong with you?" she snaps, "I was going to explain everything; I just wasn't ready." She continued. "Your mother told me everything." James says casually.

"OK! Cool then it's over there's no problem now, right?" asked Sofi, with excitement and joy.

"Yes, there wasn't it's only that I like to know the people I hang out with."

"By the way, your mother told me you were not feeling well, you were so sad, is that true?"

"Nooo, that's ridiculous, why would I be sad?"

"Hum. I don't know, my best guess would be, you missed me."

"Don't be ridiculous." She swallows hard and her cheeks turn red

"I did miss you." James confesses

"I missed you too. Just a little bit," she mumbles fast

"A little! Seriously?"

"Yes! And stop flirting!"

Starting fresh friendship, Sofi asks him if he can join her tomorrow evening, in the same place, James smiles, accepts the proposal, and he hangs up.

"Hello, are you there?" calls Sofi's mother who has just returned home.

"Yes, mother, I'm in the kitchen," Sofi said.

Sabrina finds joy in her voice but does not ask her why she is happy, she goes to join her in the kitchen after an exhausting day at school.

"What are you preparing for us?" asked Sabrina.

"I'm making a sandwich, do you want some?"

"Yes, I'm starving."

They sit and eat their sandwiches, talking about their days to each other, but Sabrina omits to mention anything about James. Wanting to go to her room Sabrina is stopped by a challenging voice behind her. "Where do you think you are going?" Sofi asks if she has nothing to tell her.

"What, I don't think so!" Says Sabrina with a fake frosty smile on her face.

"Have you seen James today?"

"Yes, I am the principal. Remember!!!"

"Not as a director," says Sofi. Sabrina feigns confusion, and Sofi raises an eyebrow.

"OK! Fine, I was worried about you, and you didn't want to tell. What did you expect me to do?" Attests Sabrina.

"And what exactly did you tell him?"

"I told him what he needed to know."

"I was ready to tell him the truth, and now that you have told him something else how will I go about it?"

"You have nothing to tell him at the risk of losing him, OK!"

"OK!"

Sabrina hugs her daughter and tells her the sentence, that every mother is supposed to tell her child even if it is not always true, "You know I love you, right?"

"Yes, I know, but I had planned to tell him the truth, I can't believe that I've almost lost it because I couldn't handle to lose the friendship of James. I was devastated, that's never happened to me before even with that boy in my old school, remember! My first crush!"

"Are you ready to admit that you like him more than just a friend?"

"Nope! He's just my friend."

"OK! Good night."

The mother goes into her room and leaves Sofi in total confusion. She spends all her night thinking about what her mother told her, and she realizes that Sabrina might be right, but Sofi simply denies it. At eight o'clock in the morning, with a huge autumn freshness, James rises up from his bed and gets downstairs, before even going to take a shower. He joins his parents and informs them that he has a second date with Sofi in the same restaurant where he had invited her for the first time. This means that she liked his choice. When he announced to his parents, they were happy for him, but had a little bit concerned about his spending too much time with this girl. Instead of dwelling on the subject for so long the get right to it. "So! Will she always remain your friend or is there the slightest chance of something more?" Asks Samira while holding his hand. James does not know what to answer because he is in a total confusion as much as they are, he does not know what the name of their relationship is. He looks ghastly, for even letting such words out. "She's my friend, but I think I'd like it to be more than that." He finally says. The parents look at each other and smile, "Hoof! That's my son, I thought you were never going to realize that you're in love with that girl," said the mother.

"You need my car for tonight, or did it embarrass you last time when you took it?" Asked Benyamin.

"Embarrass is an understatement. And why do you still call that a car?" Said James.

"Do you want it or not?"

"No, thanks. I'll pass, and she is in charge. She invited me; she will come to pick me up."

"Suit yourself."

"I'm just kidding the car did not give me shame."

"Happy to know that you have not changed your principles, even for a girl who drives you crazy."

"Oh, she didn't?"

"You tell me!"

"You know, Sofi is very different to other girls. She gets me."

"Yes, I know, now when do we see her?"

"I don't know, I'll ask her today."

James takes a bath, and go to see Jackson, and talking to him. Jackson believes that James is responsible for his uncountable failures between him and Sofi, which might be true. Sofi is developing a strong feeling for James without realizing it. She thinks that James is a special person because he plays by his own rules no matter what the prize to win is. James pops into Jackson's room and finds him scrolling Sofi's Facebook profile to find out what she likes, and use that to be closer to her. James glances the screen, the profile of Sofi's display. Then he asks if Jackson is still obsessed with her. He replies, "I am, but she does not like me. You are the only one to whom she pays attention to."

"Do you think she likes me?" Asked James surprisingly

"Yes, of course, don't you see it? Haven't you noticed how she looks at you, how she speaks to you and listens attentively to you? I know you are always waiting for the perfect girl, and this is it. Don't screw this up."

Given that James was there to confess his feelings for Sofi; he retreats when he sees the screen. James has all the reasons for mistrusting Jackson since it is not the first time that he is attracted by a girl who has crush on James. "I need your help by the way." Jackson brings his book so that James can explain to him a Math problem that he did not understand in class.

"Look at this man, this equation wants to take me to the hospital. It's like gibberish, I don't understand anything about this." Jackson helps James with a little of the explanation he understood in class; for James to know where to start, and usually it works, but this time with Sofi in his head, he could not concentrate.

“My brain is busy thinking about something else,” says James, and he asks for a cup of coffee.

Jackson’s astonished. “Since when do you drink coffee?” he raps out.

“Since now. I learned that if you cannot unlock your memory or you have laziness, coffee helps you to think better because according to the scientists it amplifies the function of your neurons.” James responds, but Jackson is still confused because he considers that James’ body is like a temple that has never ingested an enhancer such as: coffee or an energy drink or any other thing out there. “Unless you are no longer interested in the resolution of your assignment!” He continued.

“Of course I’m interested; give me two minutes buddy.” Jackson runs to the kitchen, makes the coffee and gives it to him, and they help each other to solve Jackson’s problem. Everyone has his way of understanding things. When James has not understood a subject he never asks questions until he goes home and tries to recollect the pieces on his own, like one of his favorite teacher pointed out. “Every problem in Math, Physics or Chemistry has several ways of being resolved, not a single path to follow. It is the law of nature you have many ways.”

Chapter 4

James' Unexpected Discovery

James spends the whole day with Jackson. It looks like the lonely boy is starting selfishness like his friend. In that boring long day he did not say a word about his plans with Sofi. It is almost time to go to his tryst, so he finishes with the exercise and goes home to wait for Sofi.

Some minutes later, a car is honking outside, James advance further and looks through the window. He sees Sofi in the principal's car. James leaves his room and join her. Sofi is nervously sitting inside the car, repeating a scene of what to say when James arrives. Suddenly James pops out of nowhere at her window. Sofi feels tongue-tied as she faces him. Realizing that Jamcs is waiting for her to say something. She panics, "Anyone to introduce me?" She asks playfully.

"Haha! Funny. As a matter of fact, yeah! They are inside, wanna meet them? I have promised them to introduce you to them?" he pauses after seeing her reaction to his proposition. Her eyes go widely open. "I mean if you're OK with it!"

"Sure!" She swallows heavily.

"Awesome."

Sofi gets out of the car and walks into the house of James's ordinary family, "Mom, Dad. Look who's here!" shouted James.

The parents come out of the kitchen and see the prettiest girl they've ever seen before in their living room, "You are so beautiful, young lady," says the mother.

"Good evening, Madam and Mr. Barry."

"You're Sofi I presume! The girl whose name reverberates with a thousand voices in this house?" said the father.

Sofi infatuated; smiles and says, "Oh really!" then she looks at James who denies it, "Oh! No, Dad, please." He looks at Sofi, "I don't know what he is talking about, don't listen to him."

"Please continue, sir, I wanna know everything," Sofi said.

"I think it's time we leave, Sofi," James said. Benyamin grabs her hand and they slide in the couch. He starts telling her funny stories of James. James is concerned about what the level of his embarrassment will be if he lets her sit alone with the father, but all his thoughts vanish when Sabrina brings out pictures of young James. James's eyes bug out of his head, "Mom! You don't even know her," said James coyly. The album contains pictures of him in diapers. Sofi flips the pages, "You're enjoying yourself right now, aren't you?" said James scornfully.

"You have no idea," responds Sofi, and she finishes looking through the photos.

Mesmerized by the good time she is spending with James' parents, Sofi is caught in a moment of deep thoughts. All of the sudden she feels emotional. She had never pictured James this way: with this beautiful family and a beautiful home. A brief introduction planned for two minutes becomes Ten minutes and Ten becomes Twenty and then 30 minutes, and she likes it, but they have to go. James unhook Sofi's coat from the coat hanger, hands it to her, "Are you ready to spend the rest of your evening out of here, somewhere other than listening made up stories?" says James.

delighted to make their acquaintances Sofi smiles and hugs Samira; James grabs his coat and opens the door. At the car, Sofi asks James if he wants to drive, he agrees to drive. He turns around and opens the door for her. "Oh! What a gentleman." She smiles. As soon as they get inside the restaurant they are immediately greeted by a new waiter trying to save his job. "Welcome to Rama's." He gives them the menu and turns back. James calls him back. "I'm ready." The waiter and Sofi look at each other. "You must be starving, already?" She asked. "Yep! I'm famished. We were supposed to come thirty minutes ago remember!" James makes his order and Sofi takes the same. During the dinner, they talk about the evening they have spent with the parents of James. "I'd pay anything to have parents like yours." She says lost in her thoughts. "Ha ha…You can have mine for free." James laughs.

"Seriously, James, you are so lucky."

James sees that she is seriously meaning what she is saying, he asks her why. Did not she have a wonderful family? And Sofi gives him a look emphasizing that he already knows the answer to that question. James was curious to hear it from Sofi's mouth to see how it feels, as this could help him to know how to engage conversation with her and how to ask her to become more than just a friend, even being aware of the warning. Sofi feels a flutter in her stomach. She does not know where to start. Her face turns red. James notices it and realizes that she is hiding something because it could not be difficult for her to explain, because they had already started the subject. Then he approaches his chair near hers, slides his hands into Sofi's hands. She raised her head and her big blue glowing eyes meet James'. He sees a stark emotion swirling in her gaze. Sofi is speechless then he reacts by telling her, "Please let me finish, do not interrupt me. I know there's something you don't want to tell me, but I want you to know that you don't have to, and I promise you not to act like last time. I know you told me to never ask you to be my girlfriend. When I thought I lost your friendship, I wasn't myself, I couldn't sleep or eat properly. Sofi, I don't want to lose you, but I'm ready to take the risk of telling you that I love you and I want you to be more than my friend. And one last thing, you don't have to answer me right away, I'd wait until you're ready, you can take days, weeks, months even years. I love you."

Some minutes tick by as Sofi absorbs James' overwhelming words in silence, Sofi stays fixed at James's face for a long time, but she cannot say a word and James says, "Sofi, I finished and thank you for your attention. I think that was the hardest thing for you to do. Hold your tongue while I'm talking, under other conditions you would've jumped on me like a tree." Continued James smiling nervously.

"Because you do not usually say anything important."

"So, you think what I've just said is important?"

"Yes it is, and thanks to you for being sincere even when I advised you not to do it. But, James, I need time please, I hope you understand me, as you said you would."

"Yes, absolutely, I said it and I promise."

"OK!" She nods

Then the night started becoming awkward. Words got lost. Irrelevancy started creeping into their conversations. Sofi refuses to meet James' gaze, she is afraid to look at him in the eyes, to not make him feel the feelings she is denying and then be forced to tell him the whole truth about herself, without knowing if he will still have the same feelings he claims to have for her. She will be devastated. James looks at his watch, "Curfew?" He asked. "Nope!" She smiled. She wants to spend more time with him.

"Do you know another place, somewhere quiet?"

"Yeah, sure, I know somewhere," James accepts as always, because of his love for her.

They go in a silent and romantic environment where James goes when he wants to be alone because of his teenage sorrows.

"Wow," said Sofi, "I love this place."

She opens the door and follows James, who is already outside waiting for her to show her the whole city beneath his feet. James goes back to the car, connects his phone to the car and turns on the music and comes back to Sofi,

"The more I'm getting to know you, the more I'm surprised." She said, "I did not know you like country music. I like country music too."

"Cool, do you have any preference?"

"Yes, I listen to everything it depends on the mood. I even turn on my radio to listen to news, my friend."

"No news, it's manipulative."

James has a pretty convincing theory about journalists and social media. He thinks that the people that control the world influence them: big corporations, big organizations, rich people and most importantly, the government. Governments that collect taxes from their citizens need to show them where are those taxes going, so to justify their crimes against humanity, they tag a bad picture on the person who has discrepancy with them to show the people through social media, through journalists, the falsely painted face of that person or that country. Then in case it does not end as they would have hoped, they did not waste money on the back of taxpayers.

Sofi looks at him, excited when he explains, she finds him cute and smiles. "What?" James asks her.

"Nothing you're weird," she answers.

James holds Sofi's hand and approaches her, "Enough of this, we are wasting this magic moment," he says then looks at her in the eyes and asks her, "would you accord me this dance of Passenger's *Let her go*?" Sofi poses her head on James's shoulders and James's hands on Sofi's hip, music continues looping for a long time. Sofi raises her head with an innocent face but says nothing, she lowers her head. At the end of the song, she asks James to give her a ride home. They get in the car and leave, all along the way Sofi is sad. James thinks that he knows why she is sad, he seeks several ways to make her smile without success. Then he brings out one of the stories his parents told Sofi before they went to the restaurant and she smiles. James stops the car, kisses her on the cheek and he tells her that, "Everything is going to be OK."

Sofi smiles, then laughs and her laughter turns into tears when she thinks of what's going on in this lifetime right now; she had never experienced this life before, never had feelings like these. She has no intention of letting this chance pass, but she knows that a good relationship must be based on truth. Truth brings confidence and without that trust, love will always be a lie. James starts the car, he has to drive the car to his house and give the car to Sofi to return with it, but he does not want to leave her alone on the road. He goes straight to Sofi's to drop her at her house and walk back to his house. "What are you doing, you missed the turn?" She said

"I'll take you home."

"And how are you going to get home?"

"I'll walk."

"No! I would not let you do that."

"You don't have a choice."

"OK!"

Once arriving there, she gets out of the car and tells him to go home with the car, she does not think that her mother will need it in the weekend morning. He refuses but she insists, "You can't tell me that you love me tonight and I wake up tomorrow to find out that something happened to you because of me." She cried

"I don't have anywhere to put it!"

"Find a way, now good night."

"Good night."

The house of James contains two garages, he was just refusing to go back with the car of the principal because for him it is unsuitable. He goes in with the car and finds his parents asleep, which makes it easier for him to sneak into the garage unseen, he does not need to give explanation. He opens the garage very slowly and makes it slide inside without any disturbance. Sofi calls James to find out if he is at home yet. They stay on the phone for 30 minutes murmuring about what they lived in this evening.

Early in the morning, James brings the principal's car back. Sabrina hears a car noise outside, she peers through the window and sees her car and wonders how her car has landed outside since Sofi is still in bed. Suddenly, she sees a young man coming out of the car, she looks and realizes that it is James. She goes outside with a stunning face, "How did you get my car?"

James starts to panic, "Mmm, mm, madam damn, it is, it is..."

"I'm messing with you geez!"

"Oh! OK!." James lets out a nervous laugh.

Sabrina invites James in for a cup of coffee, but he politely declines the offer because he does not drink coffee. "A cup of tea then," she said

"Willingly," he said.

"Did you have a good evening?"

"Yes, ma'am, you have a wonderful girl, she's different from any other girl I see."

"I guess I'm lucky to have her. Please do me a favor; don't break her heart, someone who does not know her will believe she's heartless, but she is a very sensitive girl."

"I love your daughter, and I'll never do that."

Sabrina wants to tell James that her daughter is in love with him, but she knows that is not up to her to say that because her daughter might crucify her for it. James finishes his tea and says bye to Sabrina before Sofi wakes up and finds him downstairs. After he leaves the house, Sofi wakes up and comes down to find her mother seated in the living room with two glasses of drink on the table, she asks her who was her guest. "It was James, he brought back the car."

"Wow, it's too early, Mom, I'm really sorry for the car."

"You don't have to apologize, actually that was nice of you."

"How do you know it was late?"

"I heard you when he dropped you off here and you offered him to take the car which he accepted with difficulty."

"What were you doing at that time?"

"You know can't sleep as long as my lovely daughter is out there."

"Aw..., Mom, you're the best."

"Yes, I know."

Sofi confesses to Sabrina that she thinks she is in love, but she is afraid that it's never going to work out between them.

"Why, what is the matter, honey?" says Sabrina softly, and comes sits by her.

"The truth, which I didn't tell him, until he revealed his flame for me, and I found out that I love him too." She said with a melancholic voice.

"If you love someone, you will always find a way to let him know you love him," Sabrina says.

"Even if I tell him the truth it won't matter anymore because you've already told him something else?"

Sabrina reaches for her hand and gazes deeply into her eyes.

"If you really you love tell him the truth. I'm sure he'll understand."

"What! Do you want me to tell him the truth?"

"I know your father won't like it first, but I'm sure he'll come around."

"You're the best."

After a happy weekend at home, the classes start again, and Sofi couldn't wait to see James. She goes to the school, but there is no sign of James, she hurries into Jackson's classroom to ask him if he has an idea of James whereabouts. Jackson didn't see James either. As she heads back to her classroom, she sees James and she smiles. She runs towards him, nonchalantly calling over his shoulder

"Hey! I have something to tell you. And...wait! Why are you late?"

"Hello! I worked late last night; I'm listening to you unless it can wait until the end of class?"

"Cool, I think it can wait."

"OK! I hope this thing you want to tell me did not make you forget about the test today, right?"

"No, I did not forget."

At the end of class, they return to their usual place and Sofi seems cheerful despite of not being able to anticipate what kind of disaster her confession might cause. "As I told you earlier, I have something important to tell you. Well, if I tell you, I think you are going to hate me forever, but I have to tell you, I love you, James."

"I know! Oh, wait what?" said James surprisingly.

"I love you," repeated Sofi. James is speechless.

He approaches her and holds her hands, wanting to kiss her, she says, "Wait James, that's not all."

James halts and listens, Sofi is frightened by what might happen, she asks him to sit and begins to tell him that she lied to him regarding her life with a divorced mother.

"What? The principal is not your mother?" James asks.

"Yes, she is."

"What is it then?"

"It's about my father."

"What about him?"

"My mother is not divorced; she is still married to my father."

"So, what's the matter then?"

"It's that he's a high-ranking government agent, who spends his time in the most secure office in the world, inside the Pentagon."

"Oh!" James' eyes and mouth go wide for a moment. He is unable to find the exact word to express himself.

"This is what I was afraid of. Please, say something."

"Why didn't you tell me earlier."

"He does not want anyone to know he is my father; otherwise I could be in danger, so now I'll have to kill you for the sake of my secret." She laughs nervously, and James plays along.

"Please don't. I'm a good secret keeper."

"I'll think about it."

"Thanks! Sofi…why would you tell me such thing."

"Yes, because I trust you, I love you, and I've never felt the way I feel when I'm around you for anyone in my life."

"Nothing will change the love I have for you unless your father debars me to love you."

"Hahahaaa, you're really a brave man, aren't you? One word from my dad and you'll forget you love me, that's impressive."

"Yes, he's a secret agent. I wouldn't want to spend the rest of my life in a minuscule cell with rats unless you agree to come with me."

"I'll go with you everywhere you go."

"OK! Then I'll take the risk."

James is pleased, but Sofi cannot help to notice despondency in his eyes. How can he inform his parents that Sofi's father is a government agent, the same people that forced his biological parents to disappear without any trace, the same ones from which he has been kept apart since his childhood.

Chapter 5

Love and Secret

It isn't the first time that James has something in his life that disturbs him, but he doesn't have the audacity to express it at loud. This time it is something stronger than him. Love, a feeling that he had never really felt before even with Georgina, whom he thought he loved. This is beyond belief. When he sees Sofi in the aisle of the school, he loses his control; talking to her makes him forget the rest of the world; when she smiles at him his world stops moving. He begs her not to laugh because if she laughs he will not be able to withstand it.

It has been two weeks since James had the avowal of Sofi about her father. James was frightened, he still has not talked to Sofi. As for Sofi, she was taken aback by James' reaction at the news even though she did not hear from him since then. James did not tell his parents; otherwise, he could lose Sofi for good, something that he will not be able handle very well.

Monday morning, a working day of the week, with a temperature of -1 degree Celsius, snow blocking all roads. James hovers to wait for Sofi at the door of the school, freezing and gnashing his teeth, Jackson arrives waddling. "I am here, we can go inside," he says.

James peeks at him, "Who told you that you're the one I was waiting for?"

"Whom are you waiting for? You look fidgety, and you'll freeze soon, is everything OK?!"

"I, I…I'm fffine, I'm waiting for Sofi," says James, shivering with cold.

"Why Sofi?"

"Adult's business, get lost now!!!"

After Jackson leaves, Sofi arrives, "Hello, James, what are you doing out here? Can't you do whatever you're doing inside?"

"Actually, I was waiting for you, we need to talk."

"No, I'm late."

"We're in the same class, remember."

"OK! You have 60 second don't waste them."

"Since our last convers…"

"Shhhh, stop, this is not the time, and the place to talk about it."

"When and where, then?"

"I do not know, maybe never and nowhere, how about that? Now excuse me." She snapped

James gapes at Sofi as she enters into the school without any pang of conscience. Once in, she sits away from the side where she usually sits with James. She is disgruntled after having taken the risk of telling him everything about herself, especially about her father, thing she never did before. James ignored her and remained indifferent for two weeks; now he wants to talk.

James eyes scan the classroom as he arrives at the door. Sofi is nowhere to be found at least not in her usual place. He continues scanning and his eyes stop on her. Wanting to join Sofi, she shakes her head at him to not even think about it. Poor James turns around and sits at his place. A few minutes pass by and James realizes that he is sullenly aloof. Lost in his mind thinking about what to do. He asks permission to go home with the excuse of having a migraine for his defense. The teacher allows him to leave since James is not the kind of student that leaves school for no reason. Sofi looks through the space between the students in front of her to see James leave. She knows that he is leaving because of her. Suddenly, Georgina who saw the scene looks askance at Sofi; then comes and sits beside her, "What's up?" She asked. "uhg you! What do you want?" Said Sofi peevishly. "what is wrong? I just saw James leave." Asked Georgina nicely. Sofi knows that ignoring Georgina is the best she can do, trusting her is equal to trusting the daughter of Lucifer if he had one. Georgina tells Sofi that she knows she is not the best person to advise Sofi about James, but she asks Sofi to give James time and listen when he has something to say.

"Why do you care! You don't like him."

"I know James loves you because he used to love me too, but not at this point."

"Yes, I know and I love him too, but sometimes he is really incomprehensible, he told me he loves me and when I said it back, he did not talk to me during the whole break. Can you believe that?"

"Remember when you first got here, his was the lonely nerd, and you became friends because you saw something in him. You didn't care about people's reactions. All the students had their eyes on you, but only James was lucky enough to have your heart. So don't mess it up."

Georgina returns to her place.

Siting there alone, Sofi feels the slightest pang of wistfulness lost in her memory. Thinking about how the entire break she was sad only because she did not receive calls and messages from James, and when she called him he did not answer and did not respond to the messages she left him. Even her mother was feeling her sadness, but every time she asked Sofi, she denied it by telling her that everything is fine. But Sofi knew that if she did not seek a solution, her mother would call James and ask him what is wrong. She had to find a solution, but she did not know where to begin because she did not know where to start. She made her mother believe that she was going to James' place every time she leaves the house. James' parents do asked from time to time about Sofi whom they have not seen for a long time. For the first time, James was lying to his parents by saying that they decided to make it slow. It became unbearable for James, he had to do something before losing her becomes a reality. James had to choose telling his parents what torments him and hang on to the possibility of losing her or lie and stay with Sofi with the risk of putting himself in danger. It was after having taken his decision that he went to the school to talk to Sofi, who did not want to listen.

At home in the middle of the day while everybody is at school is somewhat exasperating for James, but he finds it deliberating. Sofi calls James at the end of the classes to ask him where he is. "I am at home," he says with excitement.

She wants him to join her in their usual place if he still wants to talk.

"Yes, yes. I wanna talk!" exclaimed James.

"OK, at 7 p.m."

"OK-OK, I'll be there."

"You better be."

Even an evil has a heart sometimes, after all, if it was not for Georgina, who knows how Sofi would have handled the situation. Sofi never expected to have any advice from Georgina.

It's 7:00 p.m., James is waiting another 30 minutes and he's about to go back home, Sofi minces toward him.

"What took you so long, I was about to go home," James asks disquietingly.

"I was finishing my duties, and I had not seen the time running, sorry."

"Excuse accepted, provided if you accept mine."

"Let's hear it," she said.

James asks her to sit down.

"I hope that explains why you did not call me during the whole time," says Sofi.

Sofi sits down and listens attentively. James tells Sofi that he is not living with his biological parents but with friends of his parents. Sofi peers at him.

"I was abandoned by my parents for my safety."

"What are you talking about, you are scaring me."

"I knew you'd be scared, that's one of the reasons why I was avoiding you. This is something I didn't plan to tell you, and you, telling me that your father is an agent of the government changed everything."

"What does my father have to do with us?"

"It's not your father but his position in the government. I love you Sofi, but I want this to stay between us. Your mother knows we're together and my parents know that. I do not want your father to know it and I do not want my parents to know who your father is."

She approaches and hugs him, "OK! If that's what you want, I really missed you, James."

"I missed you too."

James hugs her tightly and kisses her on the cheek.

"You missed me, and you kiss me on the cheek. Come and kiss me on the lips," says Sofi.

James is chary of doing it, afraid maybe to bite her. Asked Sofi, "Have you ever kissed a girl before?"

"Yes, of course, have you ever seen someone of my age who has never kissed a girl?"

"Yes, you," she responded deliberately

"I did."

"No you did not! I don't believe you. OK! How many times?" asked Sofi, provocatively.

"Unaccountable."

"How was it?"

"Wow, I'm vexed, but anyway you can teach now, right?"

"If you promise me to be gentle," she whispered against his lips.

The lovers lay on their back in the grass contemplating the sky starlight and talking.

Sofi stops talking and begins to ponder about the conversation that she had with Georgina while James keeps excitedly babbling on and on. Suddenly he stops and peers at her. "Are you listening to me?" he says.

"I'm sorry I was just thinking…you know there are people who can surprise you in circumstances you do not expect?"

"What are you talking about?"

"This morning, after you left class, for whatever reason that was for, you really hurt my feelings you know? I did not want to talk to you and guess what happened after you left?"

"You cried?"

"Don't get too cocky now."

"What happened?" She asked

"Georgina came and sat with me as if we were the best friends in the world." She said

James sits and shows interest of knowing more. "She gave me a great advice regarding my behavior towards you at school."

"What! Georgina, cute, same high school, and she is a snake, all her actions are demoniac, is she the one?"

"Yep."

"Impressive! And by the way I don't think Jackson will be happy about us." He added

An important thing to point out. She is the girl who rejected him more than once. And asks her why she rejected Jackson.

"I dunno. Maybe because he's your best friend."

"Ohhh!" Said James, "Oh dear, is it what I think it is?" James says surprisingly.

"Maybe, tell me, what are you thinking?" she goggled.

James realizes that it was stupide of him for this waste of time, "I can't believe I listened to you. Why did you tell me to never think about asking you on a date, insinuating that would never happen?"

"I wanted to see if you'd dare."

"And..." He stirs his head, eyes wide open.

"I think you already have your answer to that since you're on top of me right now, and you don't even know how to kiss."

"You are a disgusting young lady, so what did you find interesting about me?" He giggled

"You were hitting on me the first day we met, so I wanted to test you. After telling you not to ask me to go out with you, you didn't do it, and to be honest I didn't want to have feelings you, but as they say, love is stronger than everything. And you knew how to be patient. You waited until you knew that you love me and not to be with me only because you needed a girlfriend to heal your wound from Georgina's venom."

"Why didn't you wanna have feelings for me?"

"Moving around is one of my hobbies, so I didn't want to be in love with you and then in two semesters move to another state. That won't be good for the both of us."

In the middle of their conversation, Sofi's phone suddenly trills with a text notification from her mother asking where she is. Sofi reads the text and types back on her screen. She apologizes for not having informed her that she will be absent for a long time. "It's time to come home." Responded Sabrina. James sees his name and smiles. Sofi shoves her phone into her pocket and asks him to accompany her. She passes along the salutation of her mother to James and asks him that if he knows what this greeting means in the middle of the night. "Yes, I know, let's go before a little girl becomes devoid of going out for the rest of her life." James smiled widely, his eyes crinkling.

"Let's do that, and shut up, I'm a big girl."

James turns on his old car. This time the door of his car miraculously opens in one try. Sofi looks at him and smiles, "This time your car didn't want me to practice my acrobatics."

"Yep I upgraded it!" he said

"Really!" she responded, furrowing a brow.

One their way home, it is quiet in the car for a moment. Sofi is curious about James not wanting her father to know about him, but she is afraid of ruining the moment she's having. She understands that he has his reasons, or maybe she doesn't want him to think she is pushy. It is not easy to lie to a family who loves you and whom you love in return, but it is also not easy to live without the person you love, if you have the possibility to be with that person. James drops Sofi at the door, wishes her good night. Some moments later, Sofi calls him to find out if he arrived at home safely. They spend the whole night on the phone.

The next day at school, James meets Jackson and without any dodge, he tells him all about his fabulous love story before he discovers it otherwise, Jackson seems excited to know what happened, how his soiree with her was. James remains leery, James has an objectionable cageyness sometimes, so he simplifies the answer by saying, "Nothing special." The only thing that happened is they just talked. It was the only thing missing between them, to sit and talk. Jackson tells him that he is happy for him, without knowing that this is the phrase James hates the most of all the sentences. He looks at him attentively and ends up telling him the story. And then he says, "Thank you for being happy for me." and they move along into the classroom.

Since that day, James and Sofi do not have reason to hide their feelings, even in the corridor of the school they kiss. James switched personalities from nerd to the coolest boy in school. With Sofi's help James is now able to communicate with normal people. He speaks up without considering the consequences, and that's the thing he can do the most. Before James started seeing Sofi, his parents always reminded him that people don't think the way he thinks. If he wanted to have company in his life other than Jackson he always has to talk less and listen more, but with Sofi he does not have that kind of pressure. He can be himself the nerdy whey-faced boy that he is. James never believed in anything other than science and religion, all the rest didn't matter; he did not know the feeling that someone can feel after hearing an uncomfortable truth, until he sets eyes on Sofi.

Jackson throws a party for James and Sofi. It's not every day your geek best friend gets out from friend zone after long time of trying until called failure. James asks Sofi who has a difficulty answering since she has broken his heart once. James does not insist, he says they are not obligated to go, Sofi agrees and she proposed to invite Georgina. "Wow, it looks like you have a new friend, don't you?" asks James

"Yes, you know she's not as bad as everyone think."

Sofi joins Georgina at her usual place sitting with her acolytes. Sofi inhales a deep breath and walks over to Georgina and her minions. They stare at her coming towards her. Suddenly, their conversation volatizes into the emptiness as she arrives. "Hey Georgina!" Says Sofi. "Hi!" responds Georgina, as her friends give Sofi an unwavering look. Sofi is somehow discomforted by the challenging looks given to her by Georgina's minions. "So…what's up?" Finally asked Georgina. Sofi turns around shuffles back to join James. "She has plans," she says and lowers her head. James smiles, "You didn't ask, did you?" "No, I didn't, oh my God, I froze. I've never frozen in front of someone before I swear. I just stood there blank." Sofi is in awe

"OK! Are you sure you want to go?"

"Why this question?"

"You think I don't know what you're doing? You do not wanna to be there. You're just doing it for me, and if you have to do it you want to have a friend with you, is not it?"

"You're dangerous for society, you know that?"

"No, you're the first one to tell me that, but do not worry there will be other girls there."

"And why didn't you fell to mention that before I go humiliate myself?"

"I didn't know it was important., and to be honest I wanted to see you in action with Georgi"

"Seriously, that girl is a witch and those minions, uhgr, they give me the willies."

At Jackson's, James and Sofi realized that the party is adults' type. James asks about Jackson's friends.

"They've just called me, they're on their way." Jackson says and takes Sofi's coat.

After a while Jackson's friends arrive Ricky, Nicole and Sam and their girlfriends.

"Sofi, these are my friends; Ricky the selfish one, Nicole the thicky, and Sam the goofy, they are very nice," says Jackson.

"And this is our friend Jackson the crabby," says Nicole. The party is atmospheric. Jack's friends have dropped out of school to become professional soccer players. Waiting for an opportunity that never came now they are working at Nicole's father's 99 cent store. During the evening, Sofi makes the acquaintance of everyone and she seems to like them. After a wonderful party considering James has as girlfriend, the girl Jack wanted but didn't get things could've turned into a nightmare. Jackson behaved like a true friend. Good to mention that this have brought Sofi and Jack closer and they became good friends. The love of Sofi and James continues triumphing. They have become inseparable more than before by loving each other and keeping their secret.

Chapter 6

The End of School

The month of May is about to present itself in the small community of James. The school is about to be completed after long courses, and all pupils are excited. Among of them some are already starting their dream, which is to spend moments with the people they love where nobody could disturb them, but they have a test to finish before thinking about vacations. James and Sofi spend all their time together as if they have nothing to worry about, even their parents do not arrive at separated them a little. It is agreed by all the students that James is no longer just numeric Jedi but has also become the coolest boy of the school.

James is about to intersect Sofi, who is coming from the other side of the corridor of the school. At her first sight of him she wants to backtrack returning to where she came from but she is closer to the classroom than James, she hurtles and stumbles and falls in James' hand, without saying hello he kisses her. Sofi looks at him in the eyes, "Seriously!" she smiles, "I could have died here you know?"

James does it again for the second time. One student passes by and sees two different heads glued, and it is bothering him because his locker is blocked, "Ekhrrrrr gross, please find a room," the student says, but lost in their world they didn't hear what he says or just choose to ignore him. He stirs his head and move forward. Some minutes later, "Wow, you're a quick learner," says Sofi

"That's because I have a good teacher. Frankly believe me; I'm telling you the truth."

"OK! I hope this is a course that you need."

"I must be invincible to make you proud of me, right?"

"Shut up now, you're disgusting."

"You started it."

"It doesn't matter, come I'll teach you something else," says Sofi

"Isn't it time to go to class?"

"You started it."

"Hoooo, noooo, please."

"Never mind you don't know what you are missing."

"I don't care."

When they get into the classroom, they find a crowd blocking the passage. Sofi stalks through the crowds following James inside the classroom. "What's up?" Asks James surprisingly. One of the students point their fingers at the board. "Oh!" James said. Another student in the crowd says raucously, "What? Oh? I thought you were ready; otherwise you wouldn't be out there frolicking with girls?"

"I'm ready." He answered nervously, "It's just that, the heads you're making, it makes me…cringe." He continued.

"Whatever!" the student replied.

James is actually not ready, he must be at his best to enter to the college of his choice. While students are eagerly waiting for the teacher to explain the unforeseen schedule, the teacher steps in the classroom. Students express their feelings, asking multiple questions about the exam scheduled in a month. Having all the answers needed did not prevent the sadness on their faces. They are all well aware of that success requires determination and consistency. they must be good competitors, to avoid the risk of being ejected early and deprived of a second chance. Among these students, there are some dreamers who aim very high. For someone living in the countryside it might be difficult to compete with a student from the city, who has all the necessary assets to pursue studies. This is not the case with James, he is different from the others, he also has assets because it turns out that his parents are ready for anything that can help him realize his dreams, he is a student who loves studies and who understands the studies. His parents believe that there are several types of students, one group is those who love studies but studies don't like them, which means they do not understand what they learn at school. Some love the studies and understand what they study and others don't like something related with what is called school, so they let him guess the category of the last type of student, and let him choose who he wants to be.

At this moment, James and Sofi had already returned to their books to work, they have played enough, and it is time to study for the final exams. Some students are not ready and they are worried. They tell Georgina to ask James for help with some remedial classes. Georgina reminds them of her awful relationship with James, but considers the thoughts of talking to him. "Maybe you could ask Sofi to talk to him." Adds one student.

Sofi is stricken by a profound stupor when she receives the call of Georgina, but she does not take long to know what is worth her the honor of the call. Georgina explains the discussion she had with the other students, and Sofi is surprised to hear Georgina requesting a service from someone, specifically James. Sofi let her know that she will pass the information along to James.

"OK, thanks," says Georgina.

Sofi waits for James to come impatiently. She hears a car coming to a halt and she peers through the window to find out that it's her mother. Sabrina arrives from a meeting and she's very exhausted, but her exhaustion does not prevent her from starting a fight that she's well aware of not winning. It's about Sofi's late nights out with James. "Hey! Are you waiting for someone?"

"Yeah, James?" Says Sofi indifferently. Sabrina slides he bag on the table. "We need to talk honey!"

"What's up?" Asked Sofi casually

"I think you should take a break you and James and focus on the finales," said Sabrina nervously. Surprised by the comment of her mother, Sofi's eyes go wide.

"Why? No…we have to study together."

"By the way, are you ready?"

"No! And how could you do that!" She snapped

"What do you mean?"

"You could have told me at least, I'm your daughter."

"No, at school you're not."

"Fine! But as you know James values his studies more than anything, maybe more than our relationship. You have nothing to worry about mother," said Sofi cunningly. "If you say so."

Moments later, James knocks at the door; Sabrina goes up to her room to freshen up and Sofi opens the door for James. Without even stepping foot in, she asks him to guess something. Except that he doesn't know where to start. He improvises, "Your mother is not here, we are alone, and you want to take advantage of my innocence, am I right?"

"Shut up pervert, she is here."

"I heard that," said Sabrina at loud.

James shut his mouth by putting his hand on it for 10 seconds; he is so embarrassed at a point of leaving immediately. He proposes to Sofi to go stay in her room, he cannot cross eyes with Sabrina. That would be too much to handle. To inform him the request of Georgina on behalf of all the pupils, she uses this opportunity to blackmail him into accepting immediately without knowing what it is. That's the condition to help him escape the humiliation that he will undergo in a moment. James is surprised by her attitude, he whispers, "I'm going to assassinate you."

"Time's running baby! she arrives in two seconds," said Sofi, glancing at her wrist that doesn't have any watch on.

"OK, OK, OK, deal."

"Bingo!"

"What? Bingo! Looks like my grandma," says James.

"What…I am celebrating my victory, and you don't even have a grandma."

They run into Sofi's room, and Sofi closes the door, James asks what she wants, and Sofi explains to him the advantages of studying with the others. James lets out a sigh of relief, "Wow! I thought it was something like: We can't see each other until the finales are over."

"What? Wait, you have no problem with that?"

"Of course not."

"So, it means I saved your ass for nothing!"

"Bingo!" says James, mockingly

"That's my word not yours."

"I am celebrating my victory."

She starts giggling at his whimsical sense of humor, "You're so annoying. And by the way it did come up. You and I taking a break."

"What?"

"Never mind I took care of it."

Sofi hurries to talk with her mother about her big news. "Ma'am?" Shouts Sofi.

"Whachou doing?" James is distraught by the thought of facing Sabrina after the incident earlier. Before he finishes his sentence, he hears Sabrina asking who wants some tea, James wanted it, but he doesn't want to see her. Sofi goes fetch the tea. "Why didn't James come take his tea?"

"He did not want to see you, you know he's shy even before saying those kind words, I'm sure it's worse now."

"I didn't know he'd be embarrassed. I have to talk to him, I shouldn't have said I heard him."

Inside Sofi's room listening attentively, James decides to face his fear. He takes a deep breath and comes out of the room, "I think you did well, saying that you have heard otherwise, it would've been awkward if at the end I realized you heard me."

"I'm sorry for putting you in such position, Sofi and I are like sisters. We talk about everything," said Sabrina while glancing at Sofi, who is smiling. James is entranced by Sabrina's comment he shuffles slowly next to Sofi grabs her hand and says through gritted teeth, "What does she mean everything?" Sofi looks at her mother, "James wants to know how much everything is everything?" James's eyes bug out of his skull, "What the hell? This is unbelievable."

"Tell James, it's the whole shit. You tell me everything?"

Sofi starts laughing maniacally at his dumbfounded expression. "We're just messing with you relax! I told you my mom was fun." Finally said Sofi.

"Oh, you did?" Asked Sabrina.

"Nope!" frowned James, "Another lie added to everything else she told you."

"Can I have my tea now; I think I need it?" James says quickly.

All embarrassment fades away as the lonely boy sits with Sabrina. He can't believe that he has the audacity of joining Sabrina on the sofa after what she heard him say. Sofi is making the tea while her mother is congratulating James for his courage to help the students, and that they can ask for anything for the success of their studies. Flattered, he thanks the principal for her support. As soon as Sofi steps inside the leaving room; a cup of tea in her hand, Sabrina leaves. Sitting in the same couch, James and Sofi look at each other while he is sipping his tea talking quietly about life until James asks her if she believes in love.

"Yeah, I think so!" She smiles gloomily.

Finishing his tea, James is ready to leave, so he leans to take his coat behind Sofi, she closes her eyes thinking that he is planning to kiss her, she leans forward. Utterly confused, James doesn't know what to do. He is uncomfortable doing it in the presence of Sabrina in the next room, but he also doesn't want to hurt her feelings. He improvises by rubbing his cheek against hers and extends his hand to grab the coat. Sofi open her eyes, lowers her head in embarrassment.

"I think I should go now," James said casually.

"What's the matter?" Sofi asks.

"Nothing, your mother is here," he whispered and he kisses her on the cheek and runs out.

It's not in James habits to stay late out. He finds both of his parents not yet in bed. "Where were you James?" Asked Samira.

"I was with Sofi, why?"

"You know we can't sleep if you're not here, and we can't help to notice that you're not focus lately. Is it Sofi? You do…realize…you have no room for mistake if you want to attend a good college, right?"

"I know, but hear me out, OK? I've agreed to help the others students with their classes they're failing in, so they can graduate."

"Did you hit your head or something, remind me what's the first rule."

"Never catch people's attention, I know father, but please, it's for the greater good."

"That's the point, the greater good is always the thing that put you in trouble!"

"What do you mean?"

"Not happening end of discussion."

Samira feels the pain he has for not to being free all his life, and she wants him to have this one single request, so she asks James to go to his room. James runs to his room while the couple argue about what should happen. Some minutes later, they call him downstairs. "You have our permission, only one mistake and our deal is off table. caduceus, do you hear me?" Benyamin says firmly.

"OK! Commander in Chief of Forces."

"Beat it before we change our minds, you are giving me a migraine with your ranks that nobody has ever seen."

"Good night."

After an agitated night with deep thoughts, James finished making his schedule and keeps it to himself, otherwise the others will think that he wants to control everything before even the beginning. He has to wait until they discuss about what is convenient for everyone.

Upon his arrival at school, he meets Georgina at the entrance before Sofi comes. He calls and asks her to wait, which she does, and when he arrives, he nervously greets her. She looks at him confusedly reminding him that they haven't had a conversation in a year, what have she done to earn this honor today. James gulps as he tries to answer then he realizes that he doesn't have an answer and worse he feels his legs like jelly. Georgina does that to people. When you talk to her, you feel hypnotized by her demonic powers especially when she resorts to coercion. Somehow, James managed this time to spill his guts before she takes control over him. "You're the one always trying to tarnish my image." He said nervously, "I can't just let you do that. unlike others I have a dignity and I intend to preserve it." She tells him she never to humiliate him, but he started it when he refused to prevent Jackson from breaking the heart of her best friend.

James is lost in his thought, wracking his brain trying to remember what she's talking about.

"Roxanna, but she always goes with Roxy, do you remember her?" She asked

"Yes, we studied the last year together, right?"

"Yes, that's Roxy."

"And she was Jackson's girlfriend I remember that too. They were boringly in love."

"Remember what he did to her?"

"Nope, enlighten me."

"He broke her heart when she was madly in love with him. She couldn't handle it, so she overdosed and almost died." Said Georgina. James can't help to realize how her words are filled with emotions and melancholy. "You want to sit?" He asked. She sits next to him and continues. "She transferred to another school, and she was my best friend the only friend I had." She starts shedding tears. James takes her in his arms for a long time. Lost in his thoughts for a moment, James realizes that her ditzy reputation is the result of the sorrow she's been trying to drown by making other people's lives miserable.

"I am deeply sorry! I assure you that I don't know anything about this." He finally said.

"Yeah, I know now" She muttered

"Good. So are you going to apologize now?"

"Why?" asked Georgina

"For thinking I was a monster then found out that I'm an angel, and all these humiliations that I've endured every time I crossed your path."

"Don't push it." She smiled wiping her tears

"OK, OK, it's too soon. Thank you by the way for talking to Sofi."

Georgina surprisingly looks at him, "What are you talking about?"

"Don't try to be so modest now. You told Sofi to talk to me when I acted like an idiot."

"You're welcome." She smiles.

Sofi sees James from a distance and joins him; she finds Georgina sitting with next to him. She does not know what is happening, upon having the slightest glance of Sofi they change the subject and starts talking about their study schedule. Georgina thanks James for accepting her request. James plays along and points out that he knows, she doesn't need his help to get into an Ivy League school, why give herself this hard time. She smiles and rises up then leave.

Now that they are on the same page they hurry to enter in class before the teacher. Soon after they get in, the teacher follows. The teacher is flustered by excitement he sees in the room considering how forlorn their hope were the day before. "Poor choice of words, but you look happy today, would you care to share the big news?" Said the teacher plainly. An exited, goofy kid named Robert, with the neck of a chipmunk and round face like a balloon says with a squeaky voice, "James agreed to help!" Rob is not a bright kid by the way. Robert once asked the teacher if Africa is in the European continent. Anyway, the teacher is delighted to hear that and he even offers help if they need it. At recess, James sees Jackson while he was talking with Sofi; he makes Sofi wait and joins Jackson to see if he is going to deny what Georgina told him. Jackson pretends not to remember any of it, but he is certain that James won't let it go, so he confesses to have broken Roxy's heart. Madly, Jackson asks James who told him this old story.

"Is this an old story? Well, there are people who have not forgotten yet."

"Like who?"

"Like Georgina." He snapped

"Give me a break. Did she tell you that?"

"Yes, she told me and guess what! She hated me thinking that I had something to do with it. Why though?"

"I loved her and I stopped. It's not a big deal."

James gives him an unwavering look of disappointment, "I Can't believe I took you for a good guy."

He did not expect that from his best friend. He leaves without saying a word, and Jack calls him to explain himself, James answers, "Please do yourself a favor and stop talking." He joins Sofi who notices his anger.

"I don't want to talk about it," says James before she asks.

Knowing Sofi, she won't let this go. Especially when her stubbornness strikes. She joins Jackson to ask him why was James grumpy when he left. Jackson reacts the same way reacted James, and he goes back to his classroom. Two days later, Sofi receives the key of the school from her mother as promised for the studies. Quickly she lands at James' house to inform him. She finds sitting on a chair in the corner of the porch flipping papers. Sofi reluctantly comes and sits by him. She unfolds her hand and shows him the key. James cracks a smile, but Sofi notices a sad look on his face that she can't quit determine. She asks if he has talked to Jackson. "I really don't care about him," says James.

"What did he do to you, and do not tell me you don't want to talk about it," says Sofi earnestly.

James explains why hearing the name of Jackson is not worth time squander. Unfortunately, Sofi thinks that it is not a big deal and that an old story shouldn't interfere in their friendship. James narrows his eyes on her face, "I can't believe you just say that!" he said with disappointment.

"I know, I wouldn't have said it if it were me, but I also know that the real reason for your frustration has nothing to do with the victim. You're still grumpy because Georgina hated you for it believing you were aware what was going on between Jack and Roxy," she snapped angrily

James is speechless for a moment. Staring at her unable to find the exact word for a while makes Sofi realize that James just confirmed her assertion, and that makes her very furious more than before. Her heart starts pounding so hard that James can hear it. The sound of the heavy breath she is inhaling in can't go unnoticed. Even her nostrils are feeling the pain. She is hurt, she finally starts shedding crocodile tears.

"You are an asshole," bemoaning Sofi, "Tell me, do you have feelings for her?"

"I love you and only you," cried James

"Such a liar. I can't do this right now" She says and rises from the chair, and then advices him to apologize to Jackson.

The next day, James knows that losing her would be a life shattering for him, he finds Jackson in his classroom entertaining the cheerleaders with his dark twisted sense of humor. He suddenly stops when he sees James. They sit in an awkward silence for a moment. "I'm sorry for the way I reacted last time." Said James. "Excuses accepted," snuffled Jackson. Jackson thanks James for his kind words.

The first day of revision is goes well. The studies continue the next three weeks, and it seems that everyone is ready for the exam. Every student has already made his choice, which university he wants to attend. James and Sofi want to go to Harvard University, and James has another reason to reach Harvard, which is nothing, but to follow his parent's footsteps. The main reason for his choice is that he wants to know the cause of their disappearance, and on the other hand Sofi wants to accede to this university because she does not want to follow the footsteps of her parents. She is convinced that it is the university that will give her the future she has always dreamed of having. On the last day of group study, all the students thank James, Sofi and Georgina for helping them to make up in their failing the subjects. Sofi and James have not had the time to talk about their dispute regarding Jackson and Georgina because they were entitled to no distractions. It is now after the finales, and the pupils are free and happy. They are convinced that they have done the necessary to be at the institute of their choice. Unfortunately, the results are unquestionably catastrophic for some who have been stranded.

On the day of the results, Sofi's father surprised her by attending her graduation, and James unluckily did not know until he kisses her on the lips in front of him after the graduation.

"Introduce me to your friend," says Mr. Parker

"Dad, this is my boyfriend, James this is my dad. What are you doing here dad?" says Sofi.

"Nice to meet you, sir," says James extending his hand to him to Mr. Parker. They shake hands.

"Me too." He responds in a strong voice.

"Wanna go for a walk?" Asks Mr. Parker

"Yeah! sure!" She turns her head tells James to stick around for a moment.

"He seems like a good guy!" Mr. Parker muttered. Sofi smiles, "He is!" then all of the sudden she squeezes her eyes shut then opens them and looks at him.

"Wait! I told you not to spy on me, is that too much to ask?"

"OK, what do you know about him, do you know his parents?"

"Of course, I do, you want to meet them they're over there," says Sofi, "Why didn't you tell me…you are coming?"

"I wanted to surprise pumpkin," says Mr. Parker.

Mr. Parker is the director of the CIA; a tall handsome man with a chiseled face with a large suit on, always surrounded by bodyguards. He was promoted to Director not too long ago since then he became enticed by greed and power; and his needs continue to increase, nothing is enough for him anymore. That is the cause of the distance between him and Sabrina and his daughter. Mr. Parker urges his daughter to stop seeing James because he is a liar and if she doesn't believe him, she could ask James who his real parents are. Sofi's mouth drops open in disbelief. She thought her father came to support her, but in the contrary he's there to fill her brain up with doubtful and questionable memories.

"I think you should go now," she yells at him and leaves to join James, in her great surprise she sees Georgina wanting to kiss James on the cheek as a friend, while taking a picture. She misses the cheek and kisses him on the lips by accident when he returns to look behind him. Sofi gets angry and runs away to isolate herself where nobody can find her, but James knows where to find her. Once there, he hears her sobbing. When he begins to explain the misconception of what she saw. she smacks him continuously while crying. He grabs her hands then hugs her tightly until she stops fighting. She asks him about what her father told her. He slowly loosens his arms. Then removes his hands over her and walks backwards to stay away from her. Sofi approaches and asks James to reply.

"Did your father tell you to ask me?" asks James.

"What didn't you tell me about your biological parents."

"I told you they abandoned me for my safety, and that's all I know." He responded, "Why don't you go ask your Saint father how he knew about my biological parents? And what I am hiding from you since he seems to know more about me."

"Isn't it obvious? He's the boss of the major surveillance agencies in the country, or did I forget to mention that when you dumped me for not telling you the truth."

"OK! Let me educate you something! Being the boss of all surveillance agencies in the world won't tell you where my parents are, trust me you're interrogating the wrong person." He says and turns around and he walks away with tearful eyes occasioned by someone who he thought wouldn't break his heart. Sofi continues to cry, she can't believe that she was fooled; she has trusted the wrong person. She's so hurt that she forgot the kiss she witnessed between James and Georgina.

After the graduation party, Sabrina is looking for her daughter who has not returned yet from the graduation ceremony. James goes with Sabrina after she told him. They go to the last place where James left Sofi and does not find her. Suddenly, James receives a call from Jackson who behaved gently to regain the confidence of James again.

"Hey, what did you do to Sofi?" asks Jackson.

"Is she there?" asks James.

"Yeah, but she didn't want me to say anything, maybe it's better to call her mom because she's mad at you."

"Thank you!" says James.

James tells Sabrina that Sofi is safe with a friend, she does not have to worry. Sabrina asks James if he has any idea of what's wrong with Sofi. "I have no idea," he responds, avoiding her sight

"I don't trust you, tell me the truth."

On the way home, James tells the story of his biological parents to Sabrina and tells her that Sofi's father is a government agent, so he did not want Mr. Parker to know who he is, otherwise it would put him in danger or his parents, if they are still alive.

"Unfortunately, he knows about me, I don't even know since when, and he told Sofi who confronted me about it."

"I'm so sorry about that," says Sabrina sadly.

Arriving at the house, James is stressed, to his parents who can see the anxiety on his face.

"Is everything OK James?" they asked.

James stay silent for a moment; the parents start to worry. Samira and Benyamin are in the kitchen the walk around the table. "What is it, Son?" asked Benyamin.

"I think you need to sit."

"Is it that dangerous?" says the mother.

"Yeah, I, I, I lied to you," stuttered out James.

"About what?" asks Mr. Barry.

"Sofi's dad is the government agent, and he knows all about me," pouted James.

"It's not your fault, son, don't worry," says Mrs. and Mr. Barry.

"It's kindddd...of my fault because I knew he was, and I asked Sofi not to tell him about us," says James.

"Oh my God, were you insane? What were you thinking?" asked Mr. Barry.

James apologizes for making a pitiless mistake like this. His parents are very worried because they know that now he is in danger and he has the right to know the truth that they've been hiding from him since his childhood. After the parents have finished making up their minds, Mr. Barry goes into a secret cell and opens the safe. He takes the satchel out like the last time, but this time he does not subtract any file, he takes them all. He shows the documents to James explaining why they were forced to hide the truth from him at the beginning. Mr. Barry tells him that it belongs to him now it's his heritage from his biological parents. They have bequeathed to him, and he must have them only when the day comes. When he is ready for college where he could find answers of everything he wishes to know.

"Now we have to go get some sleep, you can go to your room and take a look at it, or you can sleep; it's been a rough day, isn't it?" said Mr. Barry

"Yeah, good night." James goes to his room and begins to flip through the papers; he sees the discoveries of his parents. James doesn't take too much time to understand why his adoptive parents suggested him to attend Harvard University. After finishing reading he realizes that his adoptive parents were not chosen randomly, they had a duty to fulfill. James lay down on his bed tries to sleep but can't because of all these twisted thoughts running through his mind.

On his awakening in the morning he finds his mother in the kitchen and the father in the leaving room, and he asks if this is the cause why they pushed him into attending Harvard.

"What are you talking about?" said Mr. Barry.

"I read all the papers." said James.

James approaches Mr. Barry and calls Mrs. Barry to come and keep them company. Sitting between the two people he loves the most, James sits for a moment without saying anything. He looks at each of them swiveling his head from side to side glowing eyes and a pale face revealing the emotions of he is feelings. The old man tries to fight back the tears but can't, "I don't know what to say, I really don't know."

"About what?" asked Mrs. Barry.

"How to thank you for all that you've done for me, I've never knew, I've never even felt that I am adopted. You are the two best parents in the world; I don't know what to do to make you happy and proud of me. I love you so much."

"We love you too, and you know what to do to makes us happy and proud of you?" asked Mrs. Barry

"No, anything just, name it." asked James. The couple look at each other.

"We want you to go live with your cousin until the day comes for you to go at the college because you are not safe here anymore." Benyamin finally said

"What cousin?"

"Your cousin's name is John, you don't know him but he knows about you since you were a child. He'll help you with your college education." said Mr. Barry.

"I cannot move now. I mean it's too early."

"Of course you can, especially since you know what you know," said both parents

The results of the last exam have been published, James, Jackson and Georgina have been accepted in the institutions of their choice, and Sofi fails to get into Harvard University, and she decided to reach University of Utah. James can't believe that Sofi failed getting into the college of her choice.

Having accepted the proposal made to him by his parents to go spend the vacation with his cousin, he calls Sofi on her phone and he directly gets sent to voicemail. Despite knowing Sofi's anger, he does not hesitate to go to her house to announce the news and speak to her about his biological parents on the basis of the recent updates he received from his adoptive parents. He knocks at the door she refuses to open after several time of irritating noise; Sabrina open the door.

"Why did you open the door?" asked Sofi furiously. "I didn't know it's him," said Sabrina and she winks at James

"Sofi, can I talk to you for a sec?" James asks with a low voice.

"Lie to me again, no you need to leave, I don't want to see you anymore," said Sofi.

At the time James left unhappy; she slowly kneels behind the close door starts flowing tears of regret, and her mother comforts her.

"I didn't want to do that," said Sofi sobbingly.

"I know, I know baby, but I think you need to talk to him he didn't lie to you, he was just protecting you," said Sabrina.

"How do you know that, stop defending your perfect boy?"

"Go talk to him tomorrow. Trust me."

"OK," Sofi said as she continued crying.

James arrives at home furious, trying not to think about what happened but cannot as he thinks he has to blame himself for everything. He packs his luggage, and calls Georgina and Jackson to inform them that he is going on vacation the next morning. James does not forget to thank Jackson for taking care of Sofi the night before and he asks him to call Georgina and apologize for what he did, and with a voice filled with emotions Jackson replies, "I'm going to miss you buddy."

"Me too brother."

Chapter 7

The Ideal Friend

Classes are about to begin; students are excited to make new friends. For some of them, it is really different because at the moment when the others want to start a new life without the parental shell at the university by having fun, others search friends with whom to compete intellectually because their life is very precious and short to be wasted. So, they stand to see what the best thing is to do for this beautiful world and the people who live in it considering how life can be unpredictable and at time incomprehensible. After the departure of the parents who came to escort their children, the students are summoned to the common room to take notes regarding the discipline of the establishment, and the meeting between students and heads of departments which takes more time than expected.

Before classes start the next day, the students organize a welcoming party which is mandatory for all freshmen, so they can get to know new people. Caroline is on the student activities' board and she is the sweetest girl ever in addition to her popularity on campus, everyone admires her. As people are having a good time at, Caroline sees a charming boy sitting outside alone watching people go by. Playing with his phone, he sees her approaching; she sits with him. "Hello, I'm Caroline you can call me Carol, and you are?" She said with a Texan accent.

"I'm James." says James. James has become a completely different person since last year. He's been working out, eating healthy, and taking good care of himself. No more acnes, freckles on his pale face. He doesn't wear glasses anymore.

"Why are you sitting out here alone, no into frat parties?"

"Parties are not really my thing, I just couldn't sleep, and I'm out here because I don't know anyone inside."

"OK, I'd like you to come with me inside I'm sure you'll love it, and you won't make any friends by sitting here now! will y'a?"

James gets up and follows Carol inside and finds it really ambient. Suddenly, he hears a song that reminds him Sofi, he scurries out trying to hide his emotions. Carol is confused but it's pretty clear to her that it has something to do with the song. She follows him and slides next to him at the same spot earlier. She sits for a moment, "Do you wanna talk about it?" She said. "There is nothing to talk about." Responds James.

At the end of the evening, Caroline had introduced most of her friends to James among them is Michael. He like a brother to Carol. Michael is six feet two, dark skin with pretty brown eyes. He is a privileged kid who get everything giving to him in a silver plate. He loves parties. He can be cool to hang around with, but can also exasperating when it comes to studies. Michael have trust issues which have caused his lack of close friends throughout time. Michael has no remorse of taking advantage of the happiness that life had to offer him, but behind this happy face hides a dark secret. Hidden too deep that it's unnoticeable for someone who doesn't know him. when it comes to studies he is always closed behind door in his house and rarely comes out. Some student considers him as a crazy nerd.

Surprised by his egocentric behavior; James shortens their acquaintance. Being always surrounded by arrogant people; he recognizes one at first sight. Anyway, Michael is able to lead a double life without any problem. He is a reveler at a given moment and studious at another one. He is really impressive and surprisingly humble, respectful and kind to all those who know him well, but above all the most valuable ambition for him is to have a friend who understands him, sees things as he sees them like traveling in the imaginary world as well as in the real world and make comparisons. For him it is the way of understanding the world.

After getting to know Michael and some other friends James had a good time; as not expected, but he would need his beauty sleep for his first day of school tomorrow morning. The next day, James arrives in class, unfortunately, on his first day of class he is late, and he runs into Mr. Lancei Π the most hated teacher by all students, he has no tolerance for indiscipline. For them, he is a heartless human being, and if he has a heart, it must have been made of titanium.

James enters the room a little loopy from lack of sleep "Hello Mr." and the teacher standing in front of the board staring at him longingly and answered, "I think you're new, did they explain to you my rules because they always do it to new students before I do. They think I'm a monster."

"No sir, I apologize for interrupting, and I promise you that it will never happen again."

"Great! Starting lies your first day of school, that's wise. Anyway, it does not matter, you can sit down since it is the last time this is happening, unless you are my second favorite student."

"OK, thank you." He sits, "Who is your first favorite student sir?"

"You'll know that soon."

"OK!!!"

"Now, where were we?"

At the end of class, James crosses the path of Carol, the chatty girl from last night in the cafeteria and she proposes to him to come keep them company at their table with her friend Michael. All the other students stare at him because of what happened in the classroom in the morning. He is the only one not to be reprimanded for his interruption by the teacher. They all feel that he has something special. His first day to arrive, he is already in the yard of the great, and he has become a friend of Michael what so many of them desperately wanted but have not had the chance. After a long conversation, he asks Carol while she is a member of the comity of the school, how to access a sports group. In addition to his incomparable brain that he did not want to unveil, he is a prodigy in soccer. Carol gives him all the information he needs but intrigued she cannot keep her mouth shut. She really had to ask and hurt his feelings, "No offense dude; but I haven't seen a geek who practice sport yet. What do you do as a sportsman?" laughed Carol disdainfully

"Thanks! For not wanting to offend me, but I'm already offended, I play soccer."

"Hmm cool," she smiles.

"You don't think I can, do you?"

"To be frank, I don't believe you can even drop a ball."

"OK, you just vexed me. Tell me whom the professor was talking about when he said he had a favorite student? You?"

"Wrong answer."

"OK, do you know who it is?" he asked Michael who is sitting with them.

"No idea," replied Michael, Carol looks at Michael and smiles, Michael pretends that nothing has happened and asks his friends to go home they have wasted a lot of time in the cafeteria instead of studying. Michael stifles the conversation.

Michael is the favorite student of Mr. Lancei, but he does not like to hear a word about it. They leave the cafeteria together, but James continues towards the coach's office and explains why he wants to reach the soccer team, but the coach has doubts about his ability to play soccer because he is a computer science student. Furiously James asks the coach, "Why does everyone think that a nerd is unable to do sport. I think a nerd is better player than anyone else because soccer or any other sport requires pure knowledge of mathematics and physics."

The coach replies, "Are you insane? How is Math related to soccer?"

"To make the pass to your teammate you need to calculate the distance, and what strike force you should use by calculating the acceleration of the ball from the starting point to the arriving point after the shoot. To score a goal you need to know at what angle and how much of a degree you must bring the ball. I would say that you have a better chance of scoring a goal at the corner than in the other areas of the goal up to 90% chance."

"OK! So…I see your point. Come tomorrow."

"No, I think I've changed my mind, but I could come and prove to you my theory on the field."

"No, you won't if you don't want to be a part of the team."

"OK, I'll be here tomorrow."

"OK!"

Overwhelmed by James' theory, the coach can't wait to see James to be present at the training after he used his trick as always to get what he wants. He now knows that after making this oral demonstration he will be able to enter the team easily even if he fails the test since the coach was convinced by his speech. He goes back to class. Being late again he finds a new teacher; and a question asked to the students that requires a critical thinking. Michael wants to answer the question the teacher interrupts him, "Let's leave the question to someone who deems it necessary to keep us company at the last moment." Said the teacher. He repeats the question but makes it more. Poor James always have difficulties to express himself openly in the crowed. He is petrified everybody is looking at him silently. Seconds pass by the teacher does not ask someone else to respond. James realizes that the teacher is challenging him. James rectifies the question of the teacher and gives the best answer possible. the teacher is flabbergasted by the answer. His answer caused a mouth drop for all the student. "What's your name?" the teacher finally asked.

"My name is James Barry."

"Welcome to my class Mr. Barry."

"Thank you sir."

Class continues, and James is detecting stares devouring him from girls sitting next to him. He becomes nervous. After the class, Michael asks James, "Why did you hesitate to respond at first?"

"I'm not accustomed to showing what you are capable of openly." He answers casually.

"hum! Interesting." Retorts Michael

Michael looks at him strangely for a moment "Can I tell you a story?" Michael asks.

"Yes of course!"

"The passed semester there was a general inspection of teachers. As always whenever there is an inspection the teachers must present the course and at the end of the course the students must answer questions for inspectors to see if they understood the teacher. The teacher was Mr. Lancei and the small-minded spiteful students hated him for his severity. Being well aware that he was doing this for them they wanted him to be dismissed by pretending not to understand his courses. Mr. Lancei is married and has children, so it was out of question that he loses his job because of some rattlebrained ignorant, I answered all the questions and exposed the secret of the students. Since that day I have become Mr. Lancei's favorite and the enemy of others. You see, people in this modern world use all their means to ruin innocents' lives for no reason and it makes me angry. That is why I don't have friends."

"Wow! I figured you were the favorite, and I think it was nice what you did there. Your action was noble. Saving a man's career."

"How many people do you know here?"

"Everybody."

"Do you really know everyone?"

Michael nods.

"Did not hack into the university network because it's forbidden, you know that right?"

"I would like to say no, but I did it and you say it to someone, I'll murder you."

"OK!"

Michael has just met his soul mate. James asks Michael how it happens that Carol loves him so much but like a brother, how did they know each other. When he tells him that they've grown together, James wants a story and Michael answered, "You've had too much of stories today. We should save for next time."

James replies, "We have time."

"No, I don't have time, why do you insist are you already in love with her?"

"No, no! It's just the way you care for each other, I like it."

"See you buddy." Says Michael indifferently and walks away.

"You won't dodge the subject for ever Mike." He shouts out loud, and Michael erases his words away with a wave of his hand.

As James turns around to head home and wait for his cousin, he gets startled by the honk of a car behind him. It's his cousin in a white Lamborghini. James squints and peers inside the car. "What took you so long?"

"The traffic."

"OK are we going to have this lunch or not? I'm starving, nice car by the way."

"Thanks! Jump in."

In direction of the city, the cousins talk about their different lives in their different environments, John is the one who is paying James's charges for school and living, he is married and has a child. Being a good entrepreneur he is a doctor in pharmacy, in possession of several pharmacies and shareholder in two large factories of pharmaceutical product. Since the death of his father, John has the control of the empire. He became very close to James since he saw him, he makes sure that James always gets what he needs, but James does not accept to appear with him in public for security reasons. Once at the restaurant around their table eating their meal it is a time for James to tell his life on campus.

"How is it going; did you make any friends?" asked John.

James answers, "Yes, I have two and they are really formidable Michael, an angel face because of his cuteness and intelligence and Caroline who suggested me to call her Carol because Caroline seems like an old lady for her, she is a beautiful smart girl as well as caring."

"Wow! My cousin has friends, I can't believe my ears."

"Why?"

"I remember you telling me that it was not in your politics to make friends that it would make you weak and make you forget your goal. I am proud of you; you're making progress."

"Deeeeee! Noooo, there is nothing between us; she is just a friend and she is the first to reach out to me when I landed with my loneliness. Wanna come see me play soccer tomorrow?"

"No, you know I can't. I have a plane to take tonight, otherwise Yasmine will kill me."

"How is she by the way? I hope she takes good care of my nephew!"

"I think they miss you too."

While picking at his plate of fries, John looks at him, "You asked me what took me so long to get here."

James nods with his mouth full. "Well…I was wondering what your favorite color was, so I got the white one."

"What are you talking about?"

"The car!!!"

"Which car, this Lamborghini?"

"What? don't you like?"

"I love it, but we talked about this, no fancy stuff, and certainly not here, it is too much!"

"OK!"

"OK! I love it, I want you to take it home with you, and use it until I get home."

"Hum! OK! That's doable, or I could take it back to the dealership."

"What? Nooo…. I prefer that Yasmine uses it once a month. I said once a month no more. Until I get back."

After resuming their eating John leaves town, and James goes to his apartment to finish his homework and have a good nap, as he has a coach to convince tomorrow.

James's phone buzzes several times. He presses the pillow over his head to reduce the disturbance of the ringing. Finally, he wakes up and realizes that he is late for school. He rushes, but alas he arrives late as always. At the door of the classroom he stands his eyes darting around for a moment. Suddenly, he catches a quick glance of Carol, who beckons him to come that she has reserved a place for him. He enters and sits without the teacher seeing him and thanks Carol. "You are such a savior," he says.

"You're welcome, it is now two weeks since we started classes and you still cannot get up early to get here on time. Why?"

"I do not think I'm still not used to live alone, it's my cousin who wakes me up."

"So I think we should call your cousin then."

"If it's a joke it's not funny at all."

"It's not a joke."

After class he goes to the soccer field where he finds the team, but the coach is a minute late. He starts running around the field while the others are sitting waiting for the coach until they find it advantageous to follow his example. The coach arrives and introduces him to the other players of the team, the coach divides them into two teams informing them all that James is a geek that they should be easy on him. James smiles and observes. The whistle is heard. The game is calm James is placed in the middle of the field and begins to lead the game, giving passes to his partners for goals, motivating the player with his wonderful dribbles. And this continues until the end some players of the opposing camp were astonished by what he was doing. The coach realizes that misjudging the nerd was a mistake. He hasn't had such a brilliant player. James has an extraordinary way of touching the ball and everyone liked to see him prove himself in the world of soccer. At the end of the match the coach is exited to welcome his new player, but has too much in his plate for the moment. He can't join the team with his overloaded schedule and that he could not allow himself to waste his precious time playing soccer. He agreed to play just because the coach had underestimated him as well as Carol. Desperate, the coach makes him a proposition. "Play for the team and you get a full scholarship."

"I don't need a scholarship; as I told you my schedule won't allow me." replied James

"But if I remember you were the one who knocked on my door saying you want to play."

"And you made fun of me, didn't you?" James retorted challengingly.

He sees Michael sitting on a bench and joins him, "Did you see the match?"

"Yes, you were great and now what's next?"

"What?"

"You were the first to go to the coach and he agreed to let you play even though you started on the wrong foot. But you showed him you have the talent. You gave him hope and you let him down! You forget that his livelihood to him and his family depends on the success of the team? Why do you do that?"

"No. Do you have his file too!"

"You don't need a file to know that a coach of a soccer team is miserable."

"Wow! That's harsh! I will see if my schedule has a breach to plug."

Michael smiles and taps James on the shoulder.

"Have you seen Carol?" Asks James.

"No, I think she went to the library, why?"

"Nothing, I'm just asking. Geez!"

"If at least you were telling the truth I could have told you where I saw her the last time."

"No, I said nothing."

Michael furrows his brows for a moment hopping the awkwardness will make James talk.

"Don't look at me like that."

"I think someone is in love!!!"

"Nope! Not at all."

"Yes! It's true I see it in your eyes."

"Then you're seriously ill."

Without knowing that she attended his play James told Michael not to tell Carol about the game and leaves to get change. In the locker room he finds a crowd waiting for him to welcome him to the team without know his decision yet. the welcome being warm and moving; he thinks about what his friend has just told him and he decides to join the team without a scholarship. Studies remains for him priority number one and the most important is to validate all the subjects if not, no sport. The coach accepts with joy, but is intrigued by the fact that James refuses scholarship. Michael admired James's gesture towards the team and the coach; he approaches and says, "You made the right decision my friend."

"We'll see if that's the right decision, and stop calling me my friend," James snapped

"Why? And how do you want me to call you?"

"I think my name will be good."

"OK! Brother, but remember you see I don't have many friends, right? Do you know why?"

"No, why?"

"There are people who will tell you that they are your friends, but it's only when you're useful to them and then they throw you like a poopy diaper."

"We are on the same boat my friend, and I have paid the price several times," retorted James

It's at that time Michael and James begin their friendship by using a thorn to pinch a finger and join their fingers to make a blood fusion and they invent the slogan "The two brothers with the same heart but from different mother, and united by a strong bond which is eternal friendship."

By the time they finish, Carol arrives, "What are you plotting, I was looking for you guys I just got your message, what is it?" she asks Michael.

James and Michael look at each other and say, "Which of your questions do you want us to answer?"

Michael improvises, "You know you're like my sister and there's something I've never told you."

"What, Michael?"

"Sit, I've never told you how proud I am of you and how much I love you for always supporting me and giving me hope for a normal life. Today, I feel better and I decided to let her go and live my life. Ever since you introduced me to your friend here James I felt the urge to live and hang on. I realized that I'm not the only one who lost someone I love, but my best friend was also in the car. I'm really sorry for taking all this time and for my selfishness." He cries, Carol approaches and hugs him and says, "You haven't done anything wrong to apologize for we all loved them. Know that I'm doing well because of you, and I also love you for life never forget that."

Giving them inquisitive gaze, James is confusedly trying to figure out what is happening. It's a story he'd never heard about before, he gets closer and hugs them both squeezes them tight and says, "Everything's going to be OK, I am here to share your grief. I've been here in moments of joy I'd be in the worst moments too."

Carol raises her head and moves her lips without a sound coming from her mouth, "Thank you!"

"Excuse me for having done it without you, but James and I just completed our ritual since you took too long to get here," said Michael.

"OK! It is my turn now; let's do this."

Carol extends her hand, and they finish the ritual. Michael rises up from the bench and leaves James and Carol together sitting and talking.

Chapter 8

Seeking the Truth

Several days pass by, and the inquisitiveness is becoming unbearable for James. He has been thinking about how to bring up the subject, but he is afraid of touching a sensible point by reminding Caroline and Michael what has happened that day. James finds that keeping silence will not allow him to know the truth about the friends of Michael and Caroline.

James and Carol are closer friend than Michael. Knowing that Carol is more open to him than Michael he decides to ask her. Whenever James wants to ask, he realizes that it's not the propitious time. One day while sitting at the cafeteria James lures Carol outside to be alone with her, not being aware of his intention she follows him without a second thought. As always James jump right to the subject, so he asks Carol what happened to their friends. Carol holds her breath, gives him a puzzled look as she smiles woodenly.

"Wow! You don't beat around the bush, do you?" says Carol and walks away.

"I've been waiting for more than a week and none of you told me a thing."

"OK, then whenever you are ready to talk, I'm here," said James

"OK, thanks do you need a ride?" asked Carol.

"No thanks I'll walk, it helps me think," retorted James.

After that day James stopped asking questions despite his awareness of Carol's sadness because he is undeniably familiar with the feeling. Finding out that he was adopted because of some people hunting his biological parents was not an easy stage of his life.

Someday-later James is doing his homework with Caroline at her house, after they have finished James was about to leave, and it starts raining stormily. Carol asks him to stay and watch a movie while they are waiting for the rain to stop.

"Great idea, what kind of movie do you have here?" asked James.

"Choose one, here I'm going to grab us some drinks," said Carol.

When she comes back she finds that he put a movie that she used to watch with her boyfriend, but she didn't panic she just sits and acts casual not to give James any opportunity to ask her something. In the middle of the movie she repeated a sentence by following the actor that she memorized while she was watching it with her boyfriend. James looks at her and sees tear of old memories flow down her cheeks. Sitting near her, he hugs her to comfort her. After longtime sobbing, "It was his favorite movie; He makes me watch it every day," she forced a smile maudlinly.

"It's OK." says James, "do you wanna talk about it?" Carol raises her head looks at him with her red face. James is mesmerized by the fall of her long blond lashes over her deep blue emotional eyes. He tries to retract his question, but she starts talking.

"It was one night, at midnight to be specific. I wanted to go to a party with friends, but we were late because of Steve, my boyfriend, who was a prodigy had discovered something in his computer that he wanted to show Michael before we go. Michael had to go pick him up and see what he was talking about. Michael and I weren't ready, only Gabriella, Michael's girlfriend, was ready, so she volunteered to go get Steve. At her arrival Steve explained his discovery." Said Carol, "Gabriella calls Michael and sounded terrified on the phone. The conversation wasn't over and the phone was dead, so they decided to come and talk about it afterwards. A 5-minute drive, a truck hit their car and they were found dead and the driver of the truck and the truck was never found. Michael felt guilty about it because he was supposed to go pick Steve up. The police did not find any evidence that could help them find the driver of the truck. Nobody ever wanted to listen to us about the phone call from Gabriella. Six months later after getting the computer of Steve, Michael was trying to find some evidence that could make the police listen to him, but he couldn't because the computer was locked by a strong password. I hope that he is going to find something," explained Caroline.

"I am so sorry Carol," said James.

James asks Carol why he has never heard about it since he is there. "Most of the students don't know about it. It's been 3 years now and all the rest decided to never talk about it. It has been so hard for Michael," added Carol.

That tragic accident left Michael empty he was devastated. James passes the evening to solace Carol until she falls asleep on his shoulder, and when the rain stops, he leaves after covering her with a blanket that was on her bed. Meeting the next day on campus, Carol asks James when he left and why didn't he wake her up?

"You seemed tired," said James.

Given that James's entrance to Harvard was remarkable for Michael, he needs to ask him for help to unlock the computer of Steve, but Michael is not good in asking for help when it comes to such a situation. He has no choice but to see if James can do it. Being surprised that Michael asks for help he looks at Carol who nods to him to accept.

"OK how can I help you?" asked James

"At home, in two hours," said Michael briefly and leaves.

Confused, James looks at Carol and says, "Do you know what is this about?"

"No, Michael never says anything to no one, and he is not used to ask help, he is weird."

"Yeah, I figured."

"Just be patient with him OK!"

If there is something you need to add in James's personality, it's eagerness. James can't wait to take actions when he is told something. One-hour elapses, James calls Michael and asks him what kind of help he needs. It is something he cannot talk on the phone about; he needs James to come and join him. Apparently Michael is not the only one who wary about who deserves his truth. James tells Michael if he cannot say it through the phone then he should have the decency to come because he's the one who needs help.

"Fine, I'm coming," snapped Michael.

A few minutes later, Michael is present at James's door. "What is your mysterious thing that you cannot talk on the phone?" said James.

Michael leaps in and sits down hugging his laptop.

"I have a laptop with me that I'm not able to unbolt, can you check if you can?"

"What make you think that I can do it?" asked James.

Michael emerges from the couch and opens the door to go out without saying a word. James calls him back and apologizes for his behavior. It must be something undecipherable, to be able to resist a genius like Michael. "Believe me I've pulled all the tricks I know. I've been having sleepless nights trying to crack the code in vain." said Michael desperately.

"Let's do it." James takes the computer and asks him who owns it.

"It belonged to Steve, my best friend," Michael mumbled, "And no question because you already know the whole story now."

"What?" Said James

"Drop the act, Carol told me. Even if you've asked me I would have told you."

"Ohh really, I waited days for you to tell what happened, and you didn't."

"Like you said, you didn't ask," said Michael again.

James is wondering about what he might find in the computer.

"Is this related to their accidents?" he asked.

"That's what I want you to help me figure out." Said Michael.

Michael shows James the type of programming he has developed that has been unsuccessful. James opens his computer and starts looking for code crackers that he had developed when he was in high school. He puts them into a flash driver, and he tries them one by one until one of them has unlocked the computer. Michael jumps up joyously. James gives the computer to Michael without looking at what appears on the screen. Michael enters into the files searching for something related to the call he received from Steve the night of the accident, but he doesn't find anything important. Given that Steve was Michael's best friend if he had a strange file in his computer only Michael could be able to access it. Michael opens the file, and he sees several algorithm windows that Steve had programed and saved.

"James can you check this gibberish out?" said Michael urgently.

James was in his bathroom; he rushes out realizing that Michael found something important. When he comes he sees it he asked to Michael who created that.

"It's Steve's job, he was amazing just like you, anything you ask him to do with computer he can do it. He was a numeric Jedi."

James asks him to open another file, and so on until he sees all the files. James notices a content of a file that he believes he had already seen in the documents that have left him his parents. He doesn't say anything to Michael about the code, but he urges him never to talk about it to anyone even to Carol. "Why, do you know something that you're telling me?" asked Michael to James astoundingly.

"No, I just think that you have to wait before you tell her, you don't even know what these codes are for."

"Yeah I think so."

James begins to have trails on what his parents were looking for before withdrawing from the world of science and disappearing for good, but he remains vigilant. Michael does not know what to do with the compute, because he's always been programming, but never seen that kind of thing. "We can help each other to make the lights on his," says James.

"But now I need a little nap buddy, my brain is spinning. I feel it is making a rotation in my skull," yawned James.

"OK I'll leave you to it."

"No, you can stay, it won't take long."

"I think I have to go, but I want to leave the computer here until tomorrow if you don't mind."

After Michael left, James put the computer in a safe place. He takes his phone to call Sofi, but she refuses to take the call again. After calling several times without any response he sends a message, "I will never give up?" And unfortunately, he does not receive any answer from her until he goes to sleep.

At his awakening James turns on the computer to look closely at their findings. He sees a code that could help Michael access to the college's network, and not just the surface of the site. After having seen the amazingness of the computer he decides to wait until tomorrow to explore the whole thing. Meanwhile, he looks for someone to talk to since he is insomniac, and he does not find anyone in his repertoire someone appropriate to bother, someone he could wake up in the middle of the night just to talk. Suddenly, an idea crosses his mind. He never forgot the number of Georgina he sends a message to her and by chance he receives a reply, "Hi, honey aren't you supposed to be in bed now?" asked Georgina.

"Oh, really? What about you?" James wrote to her, "Can I call you?" He continued

"Yes, if it's important," retorted Georgina.

Oh, I am miserable, and I will continue to be miserable tonight, thought James.

"Yeah, it's very important."

"OK, call me," hissed Georgina to James.

After the exchange of some words, Georgina asks what is so important that couldn't wait till morning, James start stuttering out, and Georgina says, "There's nothing important to tell me, is there?"

"What you're doing up this time?" said James.

"I'm studying for a test, you?"

"I couldn't sleep Georgy, and I am so bored. I wanted someone to talk to, but you have to study for the test, it is OK."

"We can talk a little if you want, I miss talking to you," muttered Georgina.

Georgina has always known how it stick it to James. She can be a nightmare. Georgina asks why it is she whom he called and not Sofi. James can't lie especially to Georgina. She's still gives him shudders. Hiding the truth is not an option either. "Sofi is still mad at me." He confessed. As Georgina knows his lack of friends caused by his trust issues since childhood. She strikes again.

"You want to say that I'm the only friend you have?" asked Georgina.

"No need to rub it in. We're not in high school anymore, and for your information I have 2 more, and you that is equal on 3. I'm doing well."

"No, you are not, and by the way I don't remember giving you my number?" she laughed.

"I tricked one of you idiot minions and got it long story, and I never forgot it., but I have it in my mind. You know Georgy I had always been obsessed with you."

Georgina becomes silent for a long time remembering the last semester in high school when she felt attracted to him after kissing him by accident, but she never dared to express her feelings, especially to Sofi who became her best friend.

"Helloooo, are you there?" asked James.

"Yeah, what were you saying?" said Georgina sobbingly.

"Are you OK?"

"Yeah, what's up?"

"Are you as studious as before?"

"I am trying man. Yesterday Jackson called me, I know you told him to call me and apologize."

"No, I didn't."

"Yes you did, stop lying."

"OK, you deserved it."

"Yeah, thank you, now go to sleep I have something to do," said Georgina.

"Thank you for listening, and don't stay up late."

"I won't," she hangs up the phone, and James goes to his room smiling.

Chapter 9

Waleed Alharby

James must go to the English department to enroll for some English classes, but he needs a guide, so he asks Michael and Carol to help him find the department. Unfortunately, they are busy. He has no choice but to go alone. When he arrives at the office, he crosses the path of lanky man leaving the office and asks him if the department head is in his office and the man stares at him for a moment, "Which one precisely, because I am the only chief here."

"OK well, I came to see," James said with uncertainty.

"OK tell me what you want."

"Can we go in?"

"No, tell me here if it's important we can get in together," said the scrawny man with an Arabic accent. James wonders how can it be possible for a guy like that to be the head of English department, but he explains his situation anyway, and the pretending chief of department looks at him and bursts out laughing. James is confused to see a department head burst out laughing like a child. He tries to find out why he is laughing. The man replies, "Do I have the head of a department chief?"

"I figured, first your English awful, and you have the head of a clown."

"You're in so much trouble young man, I'm the den of the department."

"Hahahah, funny."

"OK! Follow me."

James follows him in the office, and the man tells to the director that there is someone who wants to see him, "After the visit with this student you can take the rest of the day off. You know what I mean, right?" He smiled at the director and turned around.

"OK! Chief," said the director while James is looking at the man and smiling.

"Don't mind him, he is a student here for a decade now at the same level, but is a good guy with a gigantic heart."

James sits and begins to talk about his ambitions to attend the English class of his choice. He gives him all the information he needs to complete his enrollment for the class, but he still can go to class at the meantime. James is tired of being late every time. When he arrives in the classroom he sees the same man sitting at the first table, he raises his head and looks at him and says, "I wonder why you are following me?"

Mr. Yan is the English teacher, a funny and friendly teacher, who has his way of seeing the world, sometimes influenced by what he wants to hear he always finds excuses to save the reputation of what he likes or love or for what he worships even if his arguments are based on lies or don't have a credible source. He thinks that aliens have abducted him when he was a baby, and that the aliens are the ones who created the world. He could not resist answering for James. The man and Mr. Yan are best friends, they always give each other middle fingers.

"Why follow you when nobody is able to follow your trajectory, it looks like this morning you forgot you diaper." he said.

"What? Yan?" asked the man.

"You stink, man," said Yan.

"Ohhh, really?"

"Yes," shouted all the students in the room.

He puts his head under his armpit and quickly gets it out with a platypus face. "Yeah, that's true I think I forgot to take a bath since before yesterday."

Standing at the door confusedly staring at the scene, James is dumbstruck. He can't help it but to smile beamingly, "What is this class? I think I am in the wrong classroom." Wanting to return to look for another class, the teacher catches his arm, and tells him that he is at the right place, but they are like family. James cannot believe it; the students and the teacher are weird. James goes to sit down, slowly looking at the teacher and the students around him, "OK..." and the teacher asks him to introduce himself to the students.

He introduces himself and they all do the same. It's just a class of Ten people. After that James now knows the name of the man, Waleed Alharby, the funniest student he had never met before, sometimes rude, but he is a very generous man. Waleed is the least clever man you can ever meet, his skull is literally empty, no brain, and is skinnier than a child from a third world country ravaged by hunger and a yellow smile, he has curly hair. He has serious difficulties with English, he wants to reach business school one day, but he is recommended to make English his first priority. He came from Saudi Arabia and his Arabic accent impede him from progressing. He has just finished a year and half in the English department and the head of department is obliged to put him to a higher level. Everyone loves Waleed because unlike James, he has no complex of talking with everybody or doing anything if it enchants him. It is marvelous to see how everybody loves to listen his adventurous stories.

Class begins and Yan reads a sentence that Waleed wrote on the board before James came in. Waleed's sentence contains several things, but the funniest thing is that he wrote "ASS" in a place where he wanted to write "AS". James begins to laugh softly and says, "Maybe that's why he stinks, he has a problem with ass." Waleed looks at him and says, "Why are you laughing ugly chap, I knew you were behind me after I had been in the chief's office so I wrote a sentence for you, here we are kind, we welcome every new student. For you this is your welcome gift."

James becomes silent and the whole class begins to laugh. James is very embarrassed on his first day something he is very familiar with. Usually he doesn't care when he is humiliated because it is something that he has endured almost all his life in high school, but this time he really felt ridiculous. Waleed notes that James felt humiliated and he regretted to have done that, he goes to the board erases the sentence and sits down.

The professor changes the subject. He continues the class. At the end of the course, James joins his computer class and tells Michael and Carol his terrible and horrible morning that he spent in language class.

"I told you," Carol replied.

"But on the other hand, I had fun, the students and the teacher all are in the same wavelength and I liked it."

Michael asks if it's Mr. Yan. "Yes, do you know him?"

"Yes, he is a teacher, capable of the impossible, he is creative."

"I don't even know why I ask?" says James.

Carol let the boys talk and goes home; James asks her what she has to do at home so early.

"My homework, duh!" she answered.

"OK, I wanted all the three of us to go somewhere today?"

Michael tells him that he's got work to do, but he suggests Carol to go have fun. Michael is still fascinated and obsessed by the death of his two friends in the mysterious accident. Every day after classes he does not have time for anything other than to look for what really happened that day, even after having told Carol and James that he put everything behind him. He wants to confess to James what he does after classes, but he doesn't trust him enough for the moment.

"You're always busy man!" Said James.

"Another time I promise."

"OK! And you, Carol, could your homework wait? I want to have fun today."

Coming from James, this is something miraculous.

"No, sorry I have to hand it tomorrow, I have no choice."

Suddenly, Waleed appears and James calls him to introduce him to his friends. After few words of Waleed, a smile appears on Michael's face. Even the way Waleed talks is funny. Michael says to James, "I think you were right about your new friend, he's funny." Waleed takes the opportunity to apologize for making fun of him in class when James laughed at him. James tells him that he was an idiot that he shouldn't have laughed; he didn't know what was wrong with him and usually he is the one who people laugh at. Maybe being the giver instead of the receiver for once felt good.

"So, we forget everything!" Waleed said.

"Yes, we are good," James answered, extends his hand and said, "I'm James."

"Me, my name is Waleed. Nice to meeting you."

"Hmm your English is good, don't you think, Carol?" said Michael, trying to hide his smile. James asks him if he is free to go out today for a cup of tea because all his friends have things to do, Waleed replies, "I have an ampiotment."

"You have what?"

"Ampiotment." James does not want to laugh, but it's stronger than him, he lowers his head as Michael and Carol burst out laughing and Michael says, "Oh...my goodness. It has been a long time I didn't laugh at someone's vocabulary word."

The big vein trying to pop out from his forehead shows the huffiness he's trying to hide. "What is the problem with the word." He finally said. Carol rectifies the word for him "Appointment." Waleed thanks her, "I think I'll love you one day." Smiled Waleed.

"Man, I like your friend already. I think I can reschedule my work if your friend can postpone his ampiotment."

"Why not?" replied Waleed adding, "I will cancel my appointment certainly twice if she is coming."

Carol looks at the boys, "OK fine." She agrees to follow them on condition that they wait for her to finish her homework. Michael hadn't had a real smile in a long time, and when Carol saw that she liked it. They part ways to meet up later.

Moments later, James asks Michael to pick them up from Carol's house; he is there to explain something to her before they go and then they can go meet with Waleed. "Sound great," said Michael, but he asks himself, why is James doing all that, what does he want to hide? He is not like that. The problem is that he cannot spy on James because they are the same, if he tries, he'll be busted, and it will ruin their weak friendship, so he decides to ask James what is wrong. For him, this is not only the fact of having begun the language course that excites him as much there is something else. "James never have fun who does he want to fool." Though Michael.

Sometime later, Michael's car is honking in front of Carol's house; she looks through the window and tells James that Michael is here.

"OK, did you understand what I just explain to you? Otherwise we call Mike, maybe he will be more comprehensible."

"No, I understood, thanks."

"You're welcome."

After joining him at his vehicle, they go to pick up Waleed who is ready and excitedly waiting for them. From Waleed's apartment, they go to the restaurant where James went last time with his cousin, and Carol asks if he has eaten there before, James replies that he came here once.

"With somebody?" asked Carol

"Yes, why?" said James

"A girl or a boy?" Carol said.

"No, it was a man, and I am not going to answer another question."

"It's OK."

James is guessing that Carol saw him with his cousin in that restaurant, so he told her to stop asking questions because he does not want to lie, but if she pressures him he might. Michael and Waleed are clueless about what Caroline and James are talking about, so they ignore them and call the waitress. James looks at Carol and winks at her when the other two have eyes on their menus; Carol understands that James's sign means she has to stop asking more questions. "Let's choose now, I am starving," said Waleed.

"Yeah, me too," Michael replied.

They order their food and start eating. James gets an unexpected call, he looks at his phone and sees a name that he believed to no longer see on his screen, he ignores the call and his friends ask him why he does not get it.

"No call tonight, it is between friends," James said, but deep down in his heart he could never deny that he has been waiting for this call since he landed in Boston. While the others enjoy themselves talking and eating, James has lost his appetite. Carol is very attentively observing him. She thinks there is something going on with James, she intentionally spills her glass of juice on James which will constrain him to go to the toilet. "I'm so sorry," she said, sweeping his shirt with a napkin she grabbed form the table. "It is OK." He said casually

James emerges from the chair and goes to the toilet. Once in the toilet Carol excuses herself to go freshen up. The boys look at each other, but do not say anything. After arriving in the men's toilet James asks her what she is doing there.

"I followed you. And I want you to tell me what's going on." Carol said.

"You'll have to clarify your question."

"Stop, you know that won't work with me. You told me not to ask you about this restaurant as if you wanted to hide something and now you receive a call that you do not want to take because it's friends' night. I want answers."

"OK! Fine, please can we do it at home please?"

"OK! Deal. Oh! Wait, yours or mine?" asked Carol.

"I don't care."

Carol look at him oddly.

"Wherever you want, are you happy?"

"You have no idea how overjoyed I am."

She goes back to her table before Waleed and Michael make some ideas in their mind. Around two minutes later, James comes back from the restroom.

"I think it's time to go," responded Waleed

James pays the bill, and they give Waleed a ride, getting to Carol's house Michael drop her and she stands out and look at James; James looks at Michael and tells him to leave him at Carol's place, he'll walk home.

"Are you sure?" asked Michael

"Yeah, sure, see you tomorrow."

"We're just going to talk," Carol said smiling

"I don't want to know sweetie, have fun but no too much fun." replied Michael

"You too; dude drive carefully," whispered Carol, and she kisses him on the cheek.

Michael continues his way and the other two enter.

Carol's parents are absent for some days, so they will be free to talk without being interrupted. Carol takes a bath before she sits down, she proposes to James to do so, but James declines the offer, he prefers to keep his pants on while being alone with a beautiful girl. She makes tea for them, and sits in the living room. James begins to answer Caroline's questions while sipping his lime tea. They talk all night. James explains to Carol who his cousin is and why he does not want anyone to know it. About the call, he tells her that it is Sofi, his ex-girlfriend, love of his life; she called him after refusing to pick up more than a thousand of his calls. Carol asks him why she has avoided his call all this time.

"I don't think you want to know," he answered.

"I asked, right?"

"Yeah, I was stupid, but I still love her."

Carol asks him why he did not take the call when she called him.

"I broke her heart, and I still don't know what to say, how to apologies. The only thing that I know is that she is the love of my life."

"Then why did you do something that you know is going to make you lose her?"

"It is a long story for next time."

"Sure."

"I am very tired and sleepy."

Carol proposes to James to stay for the night because it is too late. James does not want to stay, she discourages him to leave at this time. After a long back and forth he finally accepts, she shows him a room, but he prefers to spend the night in the living room watching TV. Carol goes and brings blankets for the both of them because she has also decided to stay with him. Wondering about what is going to happen; he stares at her with an innocent look. "Don't worry dude, it's OK. You can control yourself, right?" she said after seeing his look.

"Yeah, I guess."

"What do you mean you guess? You have to." she said, and she sits and cuddles him. They watch the TV and continue their conversation on another subject until they fall asleep in each other's arms.

Early in the morning, Carol's parents arrive at the house. They find them sleeping, they do not know the boy, but they are relieved to find them sleeping with cloths on. Carol's father wants to wake them up for school, but the mother stops him by whispering, "Leave them alone, I think they stayed up late, you know that Carol is an early bird."

Carol raises the head, "Mom, Dad, when did you arrive here, I thought…" she said softly and quietly.

"What? You thought we were going to come tomorrow? Who is this guy?" asked her father.

"This is my friend from school, and we went yesterday in the restaurant with Michael."

"And doesn't he have somewhere to stay?" asked her mother

"That's rude, Mom. It was too late and I suggested him to stay here with me, and you left me alone in this big house; remember?"

Carol knows that James has the livelihood more than her, but she promised James to never say a word about what he explained to her.

Carol stands up and calls James to ask if he would like to go home before going to school, "Where am I?" He replied with difficulty.

She smiled, "Get up man; Get up, you have class."

He gets up and takes his shoes, wanting to get out before Caroline's mother sees him. He is not aware of anything that happened even the fact that Carol's parents are back. Carol's mother pops out from nowhere and locks eyes with James. he is embarrassed; the mother sees the scary look in his eyes she tells him to relax, "I am Carol's mom, why are you scared did you do something wrong?"

"No ma'am, nothing," he said with panic.

"Cool then, wait for Carol. She can drop you there."

The mother urges Carol to hurry, James is waiting for her to drop him home otherwise he might be late. Carol reminds her mother that her car is in the garage.

"I know, come take my car." She shouted from downstairs.

Carol walks out of her room and says, "Can you please repeat that last part?"

"Hurry before I change my mind."

She comes to take the keys and says, "I think I will often bring some friends here, maybe I'll own your car."

"Or you can be grounded for having a boy over alone all night. Don't get used to it!"

"Nothing happened." She responded peevishly.

Carol drives down the street excitedly with James and waits for him outside. James rushes quickly, and when he gets out, he gets the call from Sofi a second time. He hesitates to take it because he has not found what to say to Sofi. One step in the car; Carol advises him to pick up, maybe it's an emergency. He takes Carol's advice and picks up the phone, "Hi! What's up?" said James.

"Hi! How are you James?" replied Sofi. Sofi goes straight to the point, apologizing for not having taken his calls that she was in a bad mood. James starts the small talk while figuring out what relevant thing to say to continue the conversation. He asks her how is school going.

"Very good. You…" she said.

"Me too. I miss talking to you."

"Oh, really?"

"Why?"

"Don't start it again please? I just called you to say hi," said Sofi.

"OK. I am late for school; can I call you tonight?"

"Yeah, that'd be great."

"OK, see you then."

Carol starts the engine, and she looks at James who smiles and they hit the road. On the way to the university, she asks him if he is happy after talking to her. “Actually, I don’t know,” he replied. He doesn’t know and doesn’t understand why for the last few months she did not take his phone calls, and suddenly she acts like nothing happened. Carol tells him to be patient, maybe she forgave him for whatever it is.

“Yeah maybe,” said James.

Chapter 10

The New Girl

Waleed is a foodie guy even though he looks like someone who's never seen food before. Food is what motivates him. Every day, after class, James and Waleed go for lunch at the Mexican grill near by the campus before going back home. The suggestion is always welcomed by Waleed. "Let's go get something to eat." Said James.

"OK! I coming," said Waleed

"Really! I coming!!!"

Waleed's grammar is the worst you can ever see or hear, but he doesn't care. He's even proud of it. He doesn't hesitate to talk with anyone. For him, if you don't talk, you won't make mistakes and you won't be rectified. That means you will never improve your speaking skills. back, James sees a girl who is in his English class. She sits at the front table; she speaks English very well and she always has a niqab on her head. Waleed can't help to notice that James is distracted by something. "What are you looking at?" He asked.

"Who's that?"

"Who? The girl! She is in our class."

"Yeah, I know she is in our class, genius!"

The girl is called Rawan, she likes to be and to do what she does solo. She always sits in the front desk. During the course, she raises her hand anytime saying, "Me, me, me teacher, me." Every question asked, she is ready, and it's so annoying, so the teacher is compelled to pick her if he wants silence in the class. She never makes mistakes though.

"Do you wanna meet her?" asked Waleed, "you can ask her many questions I think, sss-she likes questions?"

"Not funny," said, James.

"I'm not joking."

"She won't talk to me. Didn't you see her, she always sits alone."

"OK! Come with me. Have you forgotten who I am?"

"No I didn't that's why I'm worried. I am not going with you. You'll embarrass me."

Without a second thought, since James refused to go, Waleed calls the girl, "Hi! Rawan, get over here."

When she arrives, he asks her if she knows this little boy (in Arabic). She answers yes that they are in the same class (in Arabic).

"OK! I am really uncomfortable now, what are you talking about in Arabic, that's rude you know?" said James.

The girl replies that he only asked her if she knows him, and she responded.

"He always takes a sit in the back of the classroom, maybe not only is he weird but also has a problem with the board," said Rawan

"No, I think he is uncomfortable with people around him," said Waleed

"Heee. Helloo! I am still here guys, and I am not deaf." James waved his hands between them.

"OK! Can I introduce you to my friend James, this is Rawan."

James extends his hand to Rawan to greet her she hesitates to shake his hand.

"Oh, my bad; I forgot to tell him that you are not allowed to shake a stranger's hand sorry," Waleed says and takes James's hand, pulls it out, "put that back." Continued Waleed. Rawan looks at him with a sad look and she mouthed, "Sorry."

"Anyway, nice to meet you, James," said Rawan.

"Nice to meet you too, Rawan how do you spell it?"

"Like you heard it, it is not Rowan but Rawan with an A."

"Wow! It's almost the same. Where are you from?"

"I am from Iran."

"Interesting! Where did you learn Arabic? I'm from California by the way."

"I grew up in Egypt and Saudi Arabia. What are you doing in English department?"

"Actually, I am a student in computer science and I just take English for fun. What about you, why are you here?"

"I am a student, second grade in medical school, but I'm on vacation, so I decided to come here." Waleed urges them to continue their conversation on the way he is starving. James invites Rawan to join them, and she agrees difficultly.

After finishing eating, James and Waleed each take out their credit card to pay, but Rawan wants to pay; the boys refuse that the girl pays the bill for them, she insists.

"Hahaha, are you gonna do this every time we invite you?" said Waleed

"Yeah, if you want."

"Cool, every day, same time." Continued Waleed

"OK!" James watches Rawan and Waleed argue about who is going to pay, and he waves to the waitress. She comes and he gives her his credit card. Leaving the restaurant James asks Rawan, "Do you go out sometime?"

"No, I don't, I am new here, I don't have friends, and I'll leave soon."

As they walk together side-by-side, James is sneaking sideways glances at her. "Can you tell your friend to stop undressing me with his eyes?" Said Rawan to Waleed in Arabic. James does not speak Arabic, but he certainly understood this sentence. James proposes her that he can introduce her to his nice friends, and Waleed confirms it in her ears, "Yeah they're very nice, you gonna like them."

Rawan doesn't want friends especially boys, "Perhaps," she said.

Waleed is intrigued by the word that Rawan just said, and James felt it by looking at his face, "It means maybe," said James to Waleed. "Ohhh! May…beee…" repeats Waleed.

Arriving at the intersection, the boys take the opposite direction while Rawan goes home; Waleed and James walk together for a while. On the way, Waleed teases James by asking him if he finds Rawan attractive because he saw the way he looks at her. With an innocent tone, he tells Waleed that it is really tempting, but he does not believe it could be possible. Waleed pretends not knowing why he thinks that way.

James smiles, "She's Muslim and anyway there is someone in my life that I cannot forget," he said.

James's phone buzzes. It's a call from Michael who wants to see him immediately. He leaves Waleed and runs to Michael thinking that it might be something important. It's the first time that James goes to Michael's house. Arriving there, he doesn't see Michael. It's a big house. He rings the bell and waits. James is standing outside thinking that Michael invited him because he is alone and bored. Seconds later, James sees Michael's silhouette through the glass door. His parents are at work. Michael lets him in and gives him a tour of the house. James is blown away by the beauty and how big the house is. "What does your parents do again?" he asked casually

"Dad's a lawyer, and mother is a doctor." He shortened the answer and goes towards his room. Michael is ready to explain to James the reason of his presence. At first, Michael shows him his photos album while talking. James suspects that there is something going on, but Michael is vaguely talking which confuses James. James realizes that most of the photos are of Michael and Carol from childhood up to the present day; he feels something bad is coming, "Did you just call me to show me your pictures?" he asked

"No, I'm just showing you how much I care about her," Michael answered without remorse.

"So!"

"Just saying."

"And, is there something you want to tell me?" James asked furiously.

"I want to warn you if you break her heart, I will never forgive you!"

Disheartened, James lets out a nervous grin hiding his anger.

"I thought we were best friends forever!"

"Yeah! I know," he admits

"Nobody talks like that to his friend and thank you for your hospitality."

Michael grabs James's hand, and he holds on to it, "Don't turn your back on me." James pushes him to let him go. Michael stumbles on the couch and gets up and punches him. Michael knows that James is too weak to fight back. Even though he is sometime in some difficult situation, he has always been against fighting. If a pacifist way doesn't work he just works away. James opens the door and leaves while Michael is staring at him disappointed that he didn't fight back. Filled with rage, James calls Caroline on her phone, "Why didn't you tell me that your friend is from the lunatic asylum?" he asks

"What?" After he explained to her, she finds it hard to believe, and she does not delay going see Michael before considering James's claims.

"We need to talk," she said at her first sight of Michael and steps inside. Opens the fridge and takes a bottle of water. She takes a sip and closes it back.

"Hi, how are you, I'm good, thanks. What were you saying?" said Michael sarcastically.

"What's wrong with you, Michael? James called me."

Michael doesn't try to deny it, and he confesses that if he has to do it again, he will. Carol looks at him and asks why he did it.

The words are stuck in his throat, he is petrified to say the wrong answer.

"I'm listening, and you better have a good reason," she said and leaning on the fridge with her arms crossed, waiting. Michael can feel her furiousness.

"Because I care about you Carol, OK!" he yelled at her firmly.

"Yes, I know that, and I care about you too." She moves towards the couch and sits, "I know, but James is not going to hurt me." A moment of silence creeps into their conversation. Knowing that Michael care about her makes her cry on his shoulder. On each other's arm for long, she asks him. "What makes you think he's going to hurt me?"

Michael knows that if he doesn't answer, she'll know that jealousy is the only answer to his behavior towards James.

He finally decides to answer that it's because he believes that James is using her until he gets what he wants.

"You are insane, how can you even think that," said Carol.

"Because yesterday I did not know what was going on in the restaurant, and after that, he went to your house together and spent the night."

"You have to call him and apologize," said Carol.

"No, did you sleep with him?" asked Michael sobbingly.

With his face becoming red and his forehead's vein wanting to pop out, his anger is not hidden enough as he wanted to. She has never seen him like this jealous before. She lowers her head and whispers, "Oh my God." He asks her what is it. "Nothing," she said and to avoid another misunderstanding she tells him that James has a girlfriend that he loves so much, "She called him, he did not take the call. When I asked him why he didn't answer his phone he didn't want to talk about it at the restaurant. That's why we went to my house. He stayed for the night because I asked him to, but we did not sleep together, he did not even think about it. James is a gentleman."

"Huh," said Michael. Since he is not used to it he hardly admits to be wrong.

Michael regrets his behavior. Judging James inappropriately was too far. Carol pulls out her phone from her pocket and calls James for Michael to apologize who he does not feel comfortable doing it, but have no choice. After talking for a moment, she passes the phone to Michael who is embarrassed remains silent for seconds trying to figure out what to say. "Are you gonna apologize or what?" Asked James over the phone. "Okay! Fine I'm sorry all right."

"Apologizes not accepted, you can't disrespect me twice in one day. You either apologize properly or hang up the phone." Continued James confidently. Carol is listening to their conversation staring at Michael, who sees a genuine concern in her eyes begging him to apologize. "I'm sorry James, I shouldn't have reacted the way I did." He improvises.

"Attaboy. That's what I'm talking about." Said James victoriously.

Michael doesn't take defeat well, but this is an exception, so he lets it slide. He hangs up the phone and escorts Carol home. On the way, a silence reigns in the car for quite a while, and Michael apologizes to her for all the trouble he caused. Carol wants to ask Michael if it is because he wants to protect her from the unknown, or it is because he has feelings for her, but she is confused. For a moment she confirmed that he was jealous but thinking about the relationship that is between them he will always act like that. As they Arrive at home she stays in the car for few minutes, and she makes Michael promise not to act like that again towards James. Michael wants to make the promise, but he thinks it's a promise he will not be able to keep because he has feelings for her that he realized just when he saw her with James. He asks Carol if they can talk about it tomorrow.

"Sure!" said Carol.

"Good night."

In the morning at the school, Carol comes late because she couldn't sleep early. She spent all night pondering at the absurdity of what happened with Michael the previous day. She is convinced that he has more than friendships feelings for her. How didn't she see it coming? Once in class, she finds that someone else has occupied her favorite place, seeing that she is heading towards him, the occupant wants to liberate the place she tells him to not move she continues towards James. She smiles at James, "Hi!" and opens the conversation, "In your opinion, why did Michael act like that yesterday?"

"I don't know, maybe he was jealous because we went to your house together."

"I already told him that nothing happened."

"OK! So much better if he's jealous, that means he likes you."

Carol pretends to not see what he's talking about, "Naaah, I don't think so. We grew up together," said Carol.

In his turn, Michael arrives, and he sits next to his two friends with a nervous look on his face. James feels the anguish in Michael's eyes. To make him at ease he suggests them to go for some air after class which they accept.

Since the English program is an extra class for James, Michael and Carol must wait for him to finish. They go hangout at the cafeteria meanwhile. James slides on the seat next to Rawan's. She looks up and looks at him in an overwhelming manner. James's shyness strikes again as always. An unreadable expression draws itself on his face. Her eyes intently on his makes him uncomfortable. Wanting to shuffle back to where he came from, he tumbles on Waleed' foot. He catches him asks him, "Where do you think you are going?" Said Waleed with a sly smile.

"Yes, where are you going?" Added Rawan

"You scared me with your eyes."

"What's wrong with my eyes, are they big? Wimp." raped out Rawan.

James feels more embarrassed. Suddenly, a flash of memory of his life in high school comes back to him, he smiles and starts thinking about last year. Waleed and Rawan look at each other, "Hey dude, are you with us?"

James comes back to the real world, "Did you just call me a wimp?"

"Yes I did, if you are not a wimp, tell me why you're scared of my eyes. People find them beautiful."

"You did not scare me, I just wanted to make fun of you, your eyes were gleaming."

She looks at him and smiles again, but Rawan rolls her eyes after James' remark.

"Stop flirting with him, Rawan?" Waleed barges in and hisses to Rawan.

"*Astaghfirullah,*" she snapped.

"Are you ready to meet my friends?" asked James.

"Not for now," she answers. Managing to find out why she does not want friends; she does not even wait until he asks, "I'm leaving soon, and I don't wanna be attached to people. I must leave anyway," she said.

"OK, but you can come and just spend some time with us." He begs her, and she wants to, but unfortunately has an appointment to repair her laptop. James shakes his head in annoyance and offers to fixe her laptop.

"You don't even know what kind of breakdown has my computer," laughed Rawan.

"Just cancel your appointment."

"OK, I don't know what you are up to. Just be aware that I won't date you if it's your plan."

"No worries, I have a girlfriend. I just want you to make friends, and have some fun for the little time that you want to spend here instead of doing me, me, me teacher," laughed James.

"Not funny dude," shouted Rawan

"meeeeeee…ho! Sorry."

"Why won't you date me?"

"You're not my type." She smiled

James clutches his hand to his chest in mock offense, "How dare you? I'm irresistible." He smiles and they both laugh. "Seriously though, why don't you date?"

"Because I'm not supposed to. Do you believe in God?"

"Of course, what kind of person does not believe in God."

"Some people don't. Anyway, I just want to say that many girls in here have illegal babies, and I'm not here for that."

"What…?" asked James

"Illegal children, you know when you have baby from someone that is not your husband. How do you say it in English?" asked Rawan.

"Seriously? OK just say I think it's just illegitimate or bastard, but the second one is kind of harsh…actually they are both harsh you should avoid as much as possible if you like your pretty face." He grins

"OK! Good to know."

"Cool."

Rawan is convinced that James will not be able to fix the problem because she has tried in her country with great computer scientists. James urges her to get up, Carol and Michael are waiting outside. Carol sees James and Waleed with a girl inside a big dress from head to toe, she smiles and tells Michael, "Do you see what I see?"

"Yes, I think our friend has lost his mind."

"Yes, I believe you; let us pray to God for help to bring him back to us," said Carol dramatically. As they are approaching, Carol and Michael start acting normally.

When they arrive James introduces them and warns Michael not to reach out her hand otherwise, he might be vexed, but Carol can, and Michael said, "Why, that's not fair. Why she gets to shake her hand and not me?"

"Yeah, I know right! life is so unfair," said James.

Rawan smiles and lowers her head, Michael stares at her thinking, "Oh my God, my friend is not crazy, but I am going to be crazy if I keep staring at her like that. Look at this creature, is she from heaven? Look at her smile."

James waves his hand over Michael's face, who is lost in Rawan's face and says, "Hehoo…do you hear me."

"Can we go somewhere?" said Waleed.

Everybody looks at him, and say, "Where do you wanna go? And do not say eat something."

"I ronno maybe eat something," retorted Waleed, "hahaha."

"You are always hungry, you eat a lot of food, but it's like the food is eating you. Tell me do you have Anaconda in your stomach? Seriously, you need to see a doctor," said James.

"No, yesterday my roommate brought his girlfriend, and I told her da I am not eating well she gave me some bills. Since I took them, I'm famished."

"Are you are always?"

James takes Waleed to a food truck to buy sandwiches while Michael and Carol get to know Rawan, but what remains mysterious is that no one knows who Rawan really is because she haven't talked about it even to James and Waleed.

"So, are you having fun?" Asked James to Rawan who's timid.

"Yeah, I think you were right, your friends are amazing."

"I told ya, I am always right."

"We will see about that," said Rawan, thinking that fixing the computer will be a challenging situation for him.

Chapter 11

The Mystery of the Girl

While having a memorable time with her new friends, Rawan receives a call from her father telling her that he was told that she is hanging out with boys. Rawan's face turns red all of the sudden, to call her back later. She pokes the switch button and puts the phone in her purse. She cautiously turns her head and looks around but does not see anyone or anything resembling what she is looking for. Curiosity is James's weakness. He always knows when something is not right around him and that's one of his strengths. He finds Rawan weird, so he asks her what she is seeking.

"Nothing, I have to go, I have something to do at home." She stands up.

"OK," said James.

"Can you give me your number; you know; for the thing! I canceled my appointment," she said.

"Yeah sure."

After Rawan left, everyone asks James what was that about. She looks liked paranoid after the phone call.

"Maybe it is time to pray," claims Waleed.

"Aren't you a Muslim?" asked Michael to Waleed surprisingly.

"Of course I am, but I can pray later. Now, I'm eating."

On her way, Rawan calls back her father, and she asks him what the call was about.

"Someone told me that you have some new friends, even boys." Said the father.

"By someone, you mean your servants."

"Stop it, you know that you can't be there alone." Said the father.

"I knew it! Did you bring someone here to spy on me after our agreement?"

"You are my daughter, it is my job to protect you."

"That is why I don't need someone behind me every time, and it is only for two months. Now please Dad, call him back."

"OK, I will tell them to take distance, and no boys, OK!"

"Seriously Dad; no boys!" said Rawan.

"OK, OK ...sorry."

"*Shukran Abi.*" Excited about her computer. She hangs up the phone and calls James to ask him how he is planning to do it. James invites her to come over to his place if she can. He could give her the address.

"That's a good idea, send me the address."

She does not want him to come over to her apartment. She receives the address and leaves her apartment. Thirty minute later, she at James's apartment, she has something there that means a lot to her. If James fixes the laptop, it would be everything she has ever wanted, but she does not want him to see it. James receives a text of her saying that she's outside.

"Wow, that was fast," He said and went to open the door.

"Yeah, I can't wait to see you do something that many experts tried and failed."

"OK, let's see. Where is your laptop?"

"Hmm." She tosses it on the table.

James takes it, "Did you drop it?" He looks at it closely.

"No, I think it is a virus."

James plugs in the laptop, he turns it on and wants to open the documents, it does not work, and the computer starts lagging. The laptop turns off 3 times. James goes to take his bag pack where he hid his high school coding. The codes allow him to hack any computer and to destroy any computer's virus. When he gets out the book and opens it Rawan wonders, *what kind of book is that?*

The book is very important to James, and even if he loses it, nobody will be able to use it because he uses his own language to write the codes. If he wants to use a number for a code, in his book he notes the number by an alphabet letter, and if he needs to use an alphabet letter, he does the opposite, and he makes sure to remember everything with his photographic memory. Sometimes he uses diagrams or ugly pictures for curious people to not pay attention to it. James goes through the pages of viruses and tries some of his methods several times, it does not work. Rawan tells him that to forget it, but James realized that it is not a simple virus sent to the computer, this one was installed by an expert. He asks Rawan, "Who else uses your laptop?"

"No one, unless my..."

"What?"

"My dad."

"What's your dad's job? Is he a hacker?"

"Hahahaha very funny. No! He's a businessman."

"OK, let me try something else."

James looks for another antivirus code, installs it in the computer and upturns it as magic some document happens to open partly, then he installs the setup in all the files and it works, the virus is deleted. James enters in one file, and Rawan rushes to close the laptop and tell James not to look at the pictures. Too late, he has already seen the family of Rawan. He asks why she doesn't want him to look at the pictures. After realizing that he saw the picture, but didn't say anything except that it's a beautiful family, Rawan inhale a deep breath, and she says, "Let me show you when I was little."

After going through all the pictures, James goes for it and just asks why she did not want him to look at them at the beginning, and then changed her mind. She replies that she was terrified that he'd sees her in an inappropriate photo, which would forbid her not to see him anymore.

"What kind of photo?" James asked.

"Like an intimate photo, duh."

"But you are not supposed to take that kind of photo, are you?"

"I'm not supposed too, but that's my laptop and it's private."

"OK. You know some people can hack your computer and download whatever they want, so be careful."

"Thanks! James you are amazing."

"Yeah, I know, but thank you for the validation," smiled James

"And funny too, I like that." She covers her mouth abruptly and her eyes grow big. She can't believe she let that slip. Squirming, James continues joking to mask the awkwardness.

"I know that too."

"Stupid."

"No, you are the only one to tell me that, anyways don't tell anyone about this OK! Please."

"No worries."

She wants to ask him if he watches news on TV or if he read newspapers, but she does not want him to suspect what she is looking for. She asked James what his hobbies are when he's not fixing computers for pretty girl, or stalking them in English classes.

"Haha...don't flatter yourself young lady." He said casually, "I don't have too much free time, but the little time that I have is for walks alone in the park; sometimes I watch movies, and I play soccer."

"Why do you like walking alone in the park?"

"Because walking relaxes me, and alone helps me think, what about you?"

"I like listening music, watching movies and news."

Rawan is trying to get his attention on the news to see what he is going to do, and fortunately for her, he follows her.

"Why news?"

"Because I like to be informed about everything."

"Do you believe in journalists and their news?"

"Yeah, you?"

"Sorry to disappoint you, I don't."

Rawan is solace; she knows now why he did not ask anything about the pictures. James receives a call, he looks at the phone, and he finds out it is Sofi. He looks at Rawan, "What? Don't look at me, take it," said Rawan.

"I'm coming right back," he said and heads to his bedroom. He takes the call, and they talk for long time. When he comes back in the leaving room he finds out that Rawan fell asleep. He wants to wake her up, but he does not want to touch her. He decides to call Carol to come and to stay with him. Her phone rings several times before she picks it up.

"Are you crazy, what time is it man?" snapped Carol.

"I know it is late, but please just come I have a situation here."

"Huuuuu, I hate you."

"OK."

She leaves her house almost sleeping on the wheel, she arrives at James's, not as cheerful as she usually does. She sees Rawan sleeping on the sofa in the leaving room.

"What is she doing here?" muttered Carol.

James does not have any secret that he keeps from Carol, so he tells her everything. He tells her that he wanted to take Rawan to his bed, and come to sleep on the sofa, but he can't touch her, and he didn't want to wake her.

"Are you serious? What about me? Don't you care about waking me up in the middle of the night? You are selfish."

"I did it because you are my friend and a good girl. God bless you honey."

"You're an idiot, it is not a problem if you just wake her up, dude."

"OK, can you stay? Pleaaaaaaase?"

"OK, then Michael will have a good reason to assassinate you. I bet you already know that, right?" She smiles

"Maybe."

James goes to his bedroom to bring blankets for them, and when he comes back, he finds that Rawan is awake and talking with Carol. Carol tells Rawan that James called her to come because she is there sleeping in the living room, and he did not want to wake her.

"Wow, what a gentleman. He did that?" whispered Rawan.

"Yeah."

At the time James was on his way to come out of the bedroom, he hears them talking about him very kindly, and he makes a noise before reaching the leaving room to make them believe that he was not listening.

Carol asks Rawan what she is doing in James' house so late. "You American's are so curious and always strait to the point."

"Yep. That's us!" She has some difficulty to say it. Suddenly, James says that he was helping her to fix her computer it has got a virus. Being so curious and vicious, Carol wants to know more, "And…?"

"And Sofi called me, I thought we were done, but I think she still in love with me," he said with a splendid voice.

Rawan smiles and looks at Carol.

"That's great," said Carol.

"She told me that she is going to visit her mother, and she wants me to go if I can."

"And what was your answer?" asked Carol.

"I miss my family too."

"Yeah right, you miss your family."

"What do you mean?"

"Nothing."

Rawan and Carol look at each other and laugh when he asks why they laugh. "Nothing," responded the girls.

James proposes the girls to have something to drink; one wants water and the second wants soda. While James is away for the drinks, Rawan had forgotten that James is not Caroline, she asks if she wants to look at her pictures. "Yeah, sure!" replied Carol.

A mistake she was not supposed to do. She opens her laptop and shows the photos to Carol who appreciates them very much, but she meets a familiar face in the pictures. She asks Rawan, who are the people whom she is in the pictures with. She seems to have seen one of them but cannot remember the exact place she saw him. Rawan upsets with the question tell her that she must be mistaking him for someone else. This is her uncle and he never leaves the country, he is a shepherd. "What? Does a shepherd looks like this in your country?" asked Carol.

"I said he never left Iran."

"I knew it."

"What?" retorted Rawan.

"I forgot, but when you said Iran, I remembered. I saw him on the TV, he is the president of Iran."

"You are insane, he is my uncle. You're a lunatic."

"OK! We can ask."

"No, no, no, no please don't do it. You are right, he is the president of Iran, but not my father. My father is the prime minister, and he is my father's best friend. Nobody can know about it, promise me please."

"Don't worry, your secret is safe with me. Does James know about it?"

"No, he does not need to know. Even you, I did not know you watch news."

James returns from the kitchen with their orders, and he finds them whispering. Wanting to know what they are talking about, he approaches, but the girls stop talking. Rawan asks James for some fun since she lost her sleepiness. Unfortunately, James has nothing special, he does not have time to have fun, so he does not have time to buy or create his own video games, but he likes watching movies, all kinds of romance or science fiction. The girls are down for a romantic movie. James goes to take a flash drive where he saved his favorite movies. He plugs the key and hundreds of movies are displayed on the screen. More than half is unknown by the girls. He suggests them the one he likes the most, he tries and it doesn't play. He tells them that it is impossible to play this film. "Un-impossible it," snapped Rawan.

James and Carol look at each other, then at Rawan

"Don't ask me about the word. I don't know." Smiled Rawan.

He chooses another movie for them, which they watch until they fall asleep.

Chapter 12

The Dilemmas

As the days pass, Rawan tries very hard to not get attached to her new friends, but unfortunately, she's already hooked to their personalities and niceness. She must go back to her country in few weeks and James must go to California to visit his parents and see Sofi. Wanting to tell James who she really is, Carol discourages Rawan from doing it because she is about to return to Iran. As it wouldn't change anything or even worst jeopardize their friendship. James goes to see Michael and Waleed at Michael's house. He finds them playing video games and turns it off. He's there about a problem that he claims to be very serious. The friends stop shouting at him, and Waleed frowns, "It better be serious." Michael joins Waleed for support. "What is the matter?" asked Michael. He stares at them, "No, no this is madness, I can't do it." He gets up wandering in the leaving room and thinking like a lost puppy.

"What's up dude?" Asked Michael

James knows that if he reveals his problem they are not going to believe, and if they do, he will look like an obsessed hypocrite. He starts fumbling, then stuttering out for a while and ends up telling them that he is really confused and he is certain that when tells them what intrigues him, they will call him all the names except the good ones.

"We are good listeners, right Michael!" said Waleed.

"Sure," confirms Michael.

James tells them that he loves Sofi, but when he gets to California he will not know where to start and the biggest problem is that he cannot get Rawan out of his head.

"Are you out of your mind?" said Waleed because he has his reason of saying that.

"I know, but it's not easy for me to take her out of my head. Have you seen that innocent creature asleep? She's an angel" Cried James

James tells them not to judge him; they either help him find a solution or leave him alone because even if he expressed his feelings to her it would not change anything.

On the other side, Rawan is explaining to Carol why she wants to leave, which is not because she has to start her medical courses, but because she is afraid of making mistakes. Carol asks her what kind. Taking a moment of reflection, and looks at Rawan who is smiling, "Wait a sec. Is it James?" She whispers.

Rawan can't resist blushing, "Yeah, I know right! That's why I have to go, and you know what! I've never had feelings for someone before. I think it is not going to be good if I stay," muttered Rawan to Carol.

Carol knows that Rawan is right. James is not the cutest guy on earth, but he does understand people and is easy to have around. Suddenly, Carol receives a text from Waleed, which says, "We have a problem."

"What kind of problem?" she typed back

"James thinks that he's feelings for Rawan, and that is not good." Carol pretends not to understand why Waleed says it's not good.

"Why isn't it good?"

"You know why."

"OK, we have the same problem here."

Waleed leaves Michael to handle James's case by sneaking out and joins Carol at her home after Rawan left.

After discussing well, Waleed and Carol confirm that more than friendship between James and Rawan is not a good idea, it could generate many consequences in the Iranian country. Waleed thinks it is a good idea if they can talk about it together with Rawan. As soon as she arrives, Waleed does not delay lecturing her in Arabic, "Don't you think I know it is not good, I know, that's why I'm leaving, it is the only solution," cried Rawan.

"Smart thinking, you are not in medical school for nothing," said Waleed with his broken English.

Rawan needs advice from her friends, but she knows already what they are going to tell her.

"Should I tell James about my feelings even when it's unfortunately only a dream?"

"Absolutely not?" snapped Carol.

Rawan turns around, looks at Waleed with a sad face.

"You know…I can make people laugh, and how to talk with people and how to have fun, but I ronno how it works with girls, Sorry. You don't needs my advice in this case otherwise you'll be disappointed," said Waleed.

Carol looks at Rawan and she changes her mind, "It might be a good idea to tell him your feelings, but it could also be a bad idea too, and she knows one thing about James and she loves him for it."

"What?" said Rawan.

"James is caring and patient and these two make him a kind person. He brought light into my life. Since he is here, Michael changed completely. I think I see why you love him." Caroline tries to convince Rawan that everything is going to be OK, but it won't.

Rawan hides from James for three weeks for fear of having to talk about the big elephant in the room until the day she planned to leave. Rawan is not ready to go back to Iran, but she has no choice. She invites her friends at her apartment to spend the last time together. James declines the offer, saying that he has something important to do. He thinks that it would be a bad idea, but Rawan thinks it's unfair that he refuses to come to her party. If there is something James is lucky for; it is to have girls that don't have the word 'giving up' in their dictionary. Rawan sneaks out leaving her guests in the apartment and goes fetch James. Once at James', she peers through the window and sees him standing in the leaving room motionless. She knocks at the door, and James comes to the door. He realizes that it is Rawan. Before he returns, she calls him. "James, I know you're in there. I saw you. Listen, I know why you don't wanna go there. Please open the door."

James remains silent for a moment, and Rawan sits, her back against the door. She starts talking about how much fun she had these past few weeks, and he deserves all the credit. She continues on and on. James sits as well and leans his back against the door listening attentively. She talks about his jokes that aren't funny, and she laughs despite the storm cloud of emotions inside her tiny body. James stands up and opens the door, Rawan gets inside and sits down, "Can I have water?" said Rawan.

By the time James goes for the water, Rawan visits the place and takes a look in James's room that is not closed. She sees James's suitcase on the bed. "Here is your water."

"Oh, I didn't know you were leaving?" Said Rawan with disappointment.

"Does it matter?"

"Yeah, it does."

"Anyway, we already talked about it, Rawan."

"Yeah, but you did not tell me it was soon, did you tell the others?"

"No, nobody."

"First, you don't want to come to my place, and second I find out you are packing your stuff. You are not the James I was talking about seconds ago."

"I did not want to go there to see you because I am scared to put you in a difficult position."

"I know that's why I wanted to have my last moment in the USA with you. Why do you think I want to leave?"

"Because you have to attend your medical school."

"Not exactly, it's because I have feelings for you too." She freaked out

"What do you mean; for you too?"

"When I told Carol that I have feelings for you, she received a message from Waleed which says that you have feelings for me. She was in the kitchen when she received it. I read the message."

Having received breathtaking news, James sits comfortably and wants to know if it is a kind of joke. "In what level do you want to know if it is true?" she said.

James wants to know everything if it is true why after she has learned that he likes her she has not given a lead. "I had feelings for you before seeing the message. I was just lying to myself which apparently didn't work."

"OK, but this is not normal, is it?" asked James.

"Nope, it isn't," She shakes her head, "Let's go have fun something else to remember 'cause I don't want to remember this sadness. Please!" muttered Rawan.

James stands up, takes his jacket and they leave the apartment.

Arrived at the house, Waleed and Michael and Carol feel bad for him to be once again into charm of the wrong girl, but that does not keep them from having fun. "Let the party begins," Carol said, "before the feelings destroy our evening."

James is not comfortable that Carol knew he has feelings for Rawan. It's not right to have feelings for someone when you are already committed to someone else. James is with them physically, but emotionally thinking about Rawan. While Rawan is simulating joy throughout the night, James's heart is shedding crocodile tears he is still thinking that she should not go back to Iran because of him, he calls her, and asks her to sit.

"Please don't do that, please," whispered Rawan with a face of concerns.

"I just want to tell you not to go back. I cannot let you do that."

"Why, I have to go to school."

"No, you still have a whole month."

Being tired of standing up, Rawan sits and places a pillow between them. The others watch the scene. James begs Rawan, but she has already made her decision.

"Do you know that I have a girlfriend?" Confesses James.

"I know that you can't be alone, everybody likes you, and more reason for me to skedaddle." Rawan retorts and smile.

"Haha, that's funny. I was the most hated boy in school all my childhood if you may know. Sometimes I was wondering what I was doing wrong for people to despise me. Anyways, you can stay, and I will be with my girlfriend."

"Do you think that is the solution? Have you thought about how I'd feel if I see you with someone else?"

"You are not allowed to date! You'll be OK."

"Do you think love knows that I am not allowed to date?"

Waleed interrupts them to request if anyone wants to dance, but in reality, it is not the cause of his presence; he just wants to advise James to respect her choice. He tells Rawan that Carol wants to talk to her. Waleed joins James. "I thought we had already talked about it," he said.

"Yeah, but this is ridiculous. Can you believe that she is leaving because of me?"

"You know it's Rawan, if she says something, she sticks to it 1000%, so you should accept her decision and let it go."

"I'm just trying not to be selfish."

"Huh! Really, how would you define selfish?" James squeezes his eyes shut in disbelief, but Waleed is still giving him an unwavering look. James realizes that Waleed has a point.

"Believe me, man, it's the best thing to do, you gotta let her go." Said Waleed. Michael joins them to do the same sermon to James, and at the end, he accepts Rawan's decision. All of them come for a group hug, except Rawan.

Before the party is over, James leaves knowing that he won't be able to bear the looks that will be given to him by his friends. He thanks them for their supports and advices. Once at home, James's phone vibrates inside his pocket. He picks it up, it's Rawan wanting to know if James could go to the airport with her. He refuses without a doubt. Sad and heartbroken all thoughts run through her mind. She thinks that he hates her for the decision she made.

The next morning, this hard feeling encourages her to go see James before she leaves even though she knows that her flight is in about an hour, so she passes by James's house and pretends to be there for goodbye and to thank him for all that he has done for her. She sees him on the balcony and waves at him to come out. He arrives stands by the door speechless, "I'm really pleased to have met you," she said with a low voice. For the first time, Rawan does not hesitate to hug a boy, she holds him for quite a while and kisses him on the cheek.

"We have to go now," shouted Caroline from the car.

She leaves James who is trying to retain his tears ready to fall down his cheeks. She did not realize how sentimental he was until that last minute of their time together. Sensible of seeing his beaming eyes; tears welled up in her eyes and she runs to join Carol into the car. All the way to the airport Carol tries to console her but no success. "Do you think I made the right choice?" asked Rawan sobbingly.

"Of course, you did honey stop crying," said Carol.

"I already miss him, I mean all of you."

"I will miss you too."

When they arrive at the airport, Rawan walks up to the waiting room and Carol goes home while James is being devoured by an inevitable grief. Speaking of travel, James receives a call from his parents.

"Of course, I already finish packing my stuff, I will be there tomorrow."

"By the way, Sofi is here, did she call you?"

"Yes."

"OK, we are waiting for you, have a good trip."

"Thanks."

He tosses the phone on the bed and continues packing after calling Carol, Waleed, and Michael in a conference call to tell them he's going home for two weeks. Given the rough time he is going through, his friends don't judge him for not telling them sooner. They all support him but do not want a goodbye by phone.

"Can we meet at Waleed's favorite place?" jests Michael.

"What do you mean?" snapped Waleed.

"Yeah, that's true, your favorite place," claims Carol.

James laugh and Waleed asks him why he is laughing, "Are you spying on me, and talking on my back," he said.

"Nothing, OK we can meet there," James said.

Moments later, they all meet at the nearest Starbucks to the university, including Waleed, who thought that they are all going to be lost. He is impressed and he manages to know how they knew where his favorite place is.

"Because you always carry a cup of coffee from Starbucks every time, duh. No wonder you're still skinny," whispered Carol

"I sssink you have to try it, it can help you to lose weight," retorted Waleed.

"Rude!" said James.

"No thanks, I am good," sparkled Carol.

Once in the coffee shop, Waleed orders 4 cups of coffee, and Carol tells him that she does not want it.

"Me neither," said James.

"Everybody is having one, no exception," said Waleed frankly.

Michael wants to try one to know what make people so attached to it. Waleed calls the manager and asks if they have a ton of sugar, the manager, who is called Bobby, looks at him and crumps his forehead, "What?"

He points his finger to Carol and says, "It's for this little girl; she would like to have coffee with her sugar."

Bobby and the customers burst out laughing. "Fine I'll have one," cheeks Carol to show him she is capable of drinking it. The cups of coffee arrive, Carol sips to savor the taste. "Not bad," she claims but judging by her platypus face, Michael is afraid to try, but convinced by James, he tries. At the end, they enjoy it.

"Were you planning to go without telling us?" asked Michael.

"No, I did not want to go, I decided it today morning."

While Michael is interrogating James, Carol is being curious about the coffee, what kind of ingredients are in it. She demands Waleed to ask Bobby what is the recipe of the coffee. "Come with me, he's my friend."

While Waleed and Carol are with Bobby at the bar, James asks Michael when is he going to tell Caroline that he has feelings for her.

"I don't know! What are you talking about?"

"Yes, you do; tell her the truth unless you want someone to take her from you. She likes you."

"You are lying," muttered Michael.

"Stop being an idiot," snapped James.

Bobby's friends come back; James and Michael shut their mouth.

"You two are so mysterious. When you sit together you communicate without nobody knowing. Anyway, can we go home now?" asked Carol.

"Yes, I'm coming with you," James smiles while looking at Michael to make him jealous.

Michael smiles and says to James, "Let me drop her off, you can go back with Waleed," said Michael.

"Sounds great," said James.

Carol looks at them, finds it weird, "What are you up to guys?" she says.

"Nothing," responded Michael.

They all come to hug James and leave. In the car, Michael wants to express his feelings for her, but he is shy and afraid of being rejected. he cannot even look at her in the eyes. Carol finds Michael uncomfortable in the car, but she remains quiet with head down, looking at her phone. Every time she raises her head, he turns around brusquely and she smiles until she is tired of torturing him. She asks him, "What is it Michael?"

"I-I-I…I want to tell you…something that I think you already know."

"What no…I don't think so."

"I don't know how to say it, but I have to tell you I have feelings for you."

"Uhh."

"Yes, I know it's awkward, but I didn't realize it until the day you spent the night with James. I was jealous and enraged, my head was spinning. I was always afraid that someone else will come to take you in front of me because I'm such a sissy to tell you that I love you."

"Tell me about it," said Carol.

"What?" asked Michael.

"I had the same feelings, but I didn't know how to tell you."

"Thank God since this happened between James and Rawan, I had the courage to tell you my feelings I was just waiting for the right time, and a good friend showed me that it is the right time. I love you, Carol."

Michael stops the car and hugs her nervously.

"I'm sorry about what I told James when he slept over," said Michael.

After arriving home, Michael doesn't waste any time to call James and thank him for opening his eyes.

"Sure, I'll call you when I get home, see you soon."

Chapter 13

The Code

As it had always been said, that true love never dies. Just two days with Sofi, James remembers how much he loves her. She makes him forget the rest of the world, including the feelings he had for Rawan. James remains discreet about Rawan, but since he is there, Sofi found out that he is very silent, she thinks that he is hiding something. This is one of the reasons that the Barry's family loves her, they still believe that Sofi is the guardian angel of James, she is always worried about him. She is the one who brings him out from the darkness. She is the first love of James, which makes them very close to Sofi. They love her as their daughter.

She knocks at the door and it is Mr. Barry who answers, and she asks if Mrs. Barry is there, unfortunately not. Wanting to return, Mr. Barry hesitates but can't help to ask what she wants, Sofi begins to grope, "It's, it's…it's girls' stuff."

"Please don't tell me y…" said Mr. Barry.

"Ew…gross I don't even wanna hear the word please, it is not, we never…you know!" she curls her upper lip in disgust.

"Ohh thank God."

"Geez…," laughed Sofi.

"Sit and tell me how I can help my little girl."

"Something is wrong with him, he is quiet since he got here, and he did not tell me anything."

"Did you ask him?" asked Mr. Barry.

Sofi tells him that James and her had an agreement, which is not to force each other of saying something they are not ready to talk about, and to respect each other's choice, but this time it's really different, Sofi had no choice but to talk about it. James arrives home after spending the day outside thinking how to tell Sofi what he has in his heart. He finds Sofi sitting in the leaving room with Mr. Barry and asks her what she is doing there.

"Hey…surprise. I just wanted to see you and talk." She stands up

"OK, good, I wanted to talk to you too."

James's father runs to his room; he smells danger coming, and he does not want to be a part of it.

"Dad you can stay, we are going out."

He takes her little hand into his and they get out. Once outside Mr. Barry calls James back while Sofi awaits him outside. He tells him to think before doing anything stupid.

"What are you talking about?"

"You are different since you got here, and I think we are not the only ones that perceive it."

"I still don't follow you, Dad," he said astonishingly

"Are you breaking up with her?"

"What! No…I missed her a lot, and I want to be alone with her, I came here for her."

"OK, fair enough. Eh! Wait a minute; what about us?"

"It's a misunderstanding Dad, I came for you, I think," Said James sarcastically and smiled.

Barry taps him on the shoulder, "I really missed you, munchkin."

"Me too, but you gotta stop calling me munchkin, I'm grown now."

"Yeah, I'll think about it. Now go, she is waiting for you."

James goes out and gives her his jacket. Sofi asks him where he wants them to go, with a soft voice, James looks at her, smiles and says, "Want to kidnap you." For James, where they are going is not important as long they are together. Soon, they arrive at the place where Sofi found out she has feelings for James for the first time.

"Wow, I missed this place," said James.

"Me too."

They get out of the car and sit on the hood of the car. Watching the city below and James asks what she wanted to tell him.

"No, you first," she smiled nervously and gets ready to find an appropriate way to handle the breakup.

James stares at her adorable lovely face and asks her how her mother is doing, and how was college. Sofi explains the difficulties she encountered at first, and how she got through their split with the help of friends. They supported her; she felt as if she were with him all the time.

"Oh really, you still love me all this time even though you ignored my calls?"

Sofi gazes at him longingly, "You hurt me James, but I still love you."

"I'm deeply sorry," said James.

James thinks it is the right time to ask if she has met someone.

"Yeah but nothing happened, I swear," she canted.

"Eh...you don't need to swear, I believe you."

"What about you?" He does not hesitate to tell her about Rawan, "By the grace of God, she was not allowed to date."

"Can you guess why?"

"Because she likes girls?"

"Wow, how did you know?"

"I guessed."

"I'm kidding it's because she is Muslim."

"Hum! Interesting!" She exhaled

After a long talk, James proposes to Sofi to make a second attempt for Harvard since the first time was unsuccessful, and he makes her understand that this is a part of the reasons for his presence and not only because he wants to see her but he no longer wants to spend a moment without Sofi.

James knows that Sofi's dream was to attend Harvard, so he only has to convince her to help her regain confidence to realize her dream.

"James, I don't want to be far from you anymore, but what am I supposed to do."

After many convincing reasons she considers the idea of trying, but the test is in about just two weeks. Sofi is not sure of being capable of doing it, but she certainly doesn't want to spend another time without James.

"Let's do it." She cheered up

James calls his cousin to tell him that he has an unexpected situation, but he will do his best to go there before going back to Boston.

"Who did you just call?" asked Sofi.

"My cousin, he lives in New York."

The last decision would be for Sofi, but she will need support from her mother and her father first before making her decision.

"So, tell me about that girl Rawan."

"Babe, you don't wanna know."

"Yes, I do."

James talks about Rawan from the first day of their encounter until the days of his trip, including the day she treated him of a wimp.

"Wow!" said Sofi.

"I hope that you are not jealous."

"I am, but just a little," smiled Sofi.

James approaches Sofi and gazes deeply into her eyes. Sofi is mortified as she waits for the following stunt that James is going to pull. It does not take her long to know. He reluctantly gives her a pec and another one, then he kisses her intensively. After an intensive kiss Sofi pulls out her lips breathlessly and asks him to stop, it is too fast. Obedient, James stop and stares at Sofi who's sitting there pondering the absurdity of how things can shift around in matter of seconds. Earlier she was thinking about how to handle heartbreak again, and now she's debating on how to handle such affection. "I think we should go home now," James interrupts her thoughts.

"Yeah, absolutely." They get in the car. On the way to go home, Sofi says, "I wanted to ask you why are you so quiet, but I wasn't ready to hear what you were going to say."

"Why?"

"I was scared of hearing that you don't love me anymore, and when you told me that you want to talk to me you increased my worries. I thought that you were breaking up with me."

"No, don't be ridiculous."

"Then what is it? Tell me."

"I'm having nightmares about my biological parents, and the thing that I see is scarier than seeing someone coming back for you from the dead."

In his nightmares he sees his biological parents wrestling against unknown demonic entities, that want to have control over something very important, but he does not know what it is, and everything becomes the nothingness of a blow. Sofi is concerned as she always has been about James, so she suggests him to talk about it to Mr. or Mrs. Barry.

"You are so witty if I tell them that they are going to worry about me," he says.

"You should talk about it though and stop torturing yourself."

James drops Sofi at her house, and she asks him if he wants to come in, maybe her mother is not sleeping they could talk. James tries to avoid the subject of going in, but as always, Sofi with her devilish tricks works on James, "You might be able to convince my mother to support me for the test to get into Harvard!" She starts to blink her eyes fast and James smiles, "You keep doing that."

"What? I'm not doing anything."

"Your eyes, Stop it."

"Are you coming?"

"OK I'm coming, are you still torturing people with your gleaming eyes?"

"Just you."

James follows her, and they find Sabrina getting ready to go back to bed after finishing with school works.

"Oh, now I understand why you didn't call me all day long," said Sabrina.

"Hi, ma'am!" said James meekly.

"You'll never change, you still have the same humble manners." Happy to see him, she gets up and hugs him.

Tired and sleepy after a long day of work, Sabrina is heading to her room, but Sofi beseeches her to stay a little longer that she has something to tell her.

She sits and listens carefully because it is not always that Sofi has something to share with her.

After listening attentively what her daughter has to say, she accepts the idea but does not think that her father will agree because he always wanted her to study where the whole generation of her family studied. She has to be there to make a place for herself in society. Sofi gets mad and goes to her room. Being alone with Sabrina, James intervenes, "Did you know that she was obsessed about getting into Harvard?"

"No, she never told me she wanted to go there." said Sabrina with a stupefied face.

"Simply because her life is controlled, and she imagines whatever she says it would not change anything. Above of all, it is because she loves you, she does what makes you happy." Intrigued by the behavior and the silence of her daughter all this time, makes Sabrina feel bad about herself. Mothers should be the ones making sacrifices to make her child happy not the other way around. She gets up from the sofa wanting to go upstairs to Sofi's room, but James thinks that it is a good idea if she lets him go talk to her. Once at her door he finds Sofi curled up in her blanket. "Leave me alone I don't wanna see anyone," she moaned.

"It's me, James, I just want to…"

"Who cares? Go away." She cried

"OK, see you," whirled away, James.

"Seriously!" Snapped Sofi.

James startled, "What! You told me to get lost."

"I was kidding; I wanted to see what you were actually going to do."

"You have a really dark sense of humor, you know that?"

"I think Rawan was right, you really are a wimp."

"We are going to see about that," said James.

He strides, trying to catch her, and she gets up and begins to run around her bed, keeping distance between them. Sabrina hears her screams and laughs from her room, she finds that letting James go wasn't a bad reasoning. Suddenly Sofi is betrayed by her curiosity, wanting to watch a message she has just received on her phone. Unfortunately, it was Sabrina who sent a message saying, "I love you, honey."

At the moment she leans to take the phone James put his hand on her.

"Let me see the message first please," Sofi begged him.

"Ohh no…seriously Mom, did you see what you just did," yelled Sofi.

"Sorry, I said I love you."

"You say it all the time mom, now wasn't a good time to say it. I got caught. Can you free me?"

Sabrina smiles and tells her not to give up.

"Stop tickling me, I'm going to pee, please James," squealed Sofi to James.

James stops and sits in front of her and tells her what he talked about with her mother. James leaves Sofi joyful and goes home.

As soon as he parks the car on the street near the house, he receives a call from Carol who wants to know how things are with Sofi. Hard for him to find the exact words to explain how he feels when he is with Sofi, he remains silent for a while.

"Are you there, weirdo?"

"It's great with Sofi. What about you, how are things going?"

"I was with Michael and he just left," said Carol.

"Humm…What were you doing at this time of the night, nasty little witch."

James reckons that Michael never leave home at night, so he kind of surprised. She shares the news with him understand that his plan worked.

"What you are talking about."

"Yeah, you do know what I am talking about. You ask me that you wanted to escort me home because you knew that Michael would get jealous. So, you forced him to get out of his cowardliness."

"Oh, cool then, right!"

"No, you are so dead. Tell me when you are coming back."

"Whatever. You wish I was there right now so you can thank me outstandingly." He laughed.

"You have no idea." She retorted.

By simple curiosity, James asks her how she feels about Michael. Her response comes from out of the ordinary in just one word "Paradise" she compares her feeling to being in paradise when she is with him. James thought he was the most insane person when he is in a relationship, but he finds out that he is the pupil of an elementary school compare to Carol.

"We miss you, come back," said Carol.

James notices that the light is lighten up in the house while sitting in the car, he tells Carol to wait, and he goes to the house, he finds Mrs. Barry waiting for him while the father is already in bed. James salutes and asks why she is sitting in the living room alone in the middle of the night. She couldn't help it considering that James is her little precious one who always needs protection, so she was waiting for him before going to bed.

"No..., Mom I am grown now, and you're too old to stay up all night waiting for me," James hissed to her.

"OK, honey if you don't stay late next time. So what did you talk about with Sofi?"

James goes to the kitchen, grabs a cup of tea and sits next to her rememorize all his night before she goes to bed.

"We thought that you were going to break up with her."

"Really! Dad told you that?"

"Yeah, he sure did, anyways, good night."

James takes his computer to look for the test deadline. He knew it was close, but not at this point. So Sofi has only 5 days to be prepared for the test.

Meanwhile, Sabrina is in Sofi's room having girls' time, "Why did you not tell me about Harvard?" she asked

"I wanted to tell you, but you and Dad wanted me to go to the university where you met. I told myself that it would serve no purpose to disappoint you, and I had not been accepted."

"Maybe this time you'll make it."

"What?"

"You have my whole support sweetie."

Sofi gets up and starts jumping, "Thank you Mom, you are the best."

Three days after rough revision Sofi feels ready to do her interview, so she fills out a form to get an admission to Harvard. Unfortunately, her form is refused several times. She calls the admissions department and gets Sarah Solano on the line to ask her what is wrong with her application. Solano asks if it is her first time to register.

"No," she answers the last semester she had tried.

"Why haven't you attended last semester?"

"Because I wasn't accepted."

"OK, your form was rejected because you had been accepted the past semester and you didn't show up and you didn't give any reason why."

"Are you sure it's me, can you read the name to make sure please?"

The Admissions Office Assistant reads the name and specific information. Having heard the name Marie Boulere, the director of the office, gets out, and asks her assistant, "Who is she talking to? This name looks familiar."

"She's a student, who had an admission last semester, but she didn't think it necessary to come, and obviously she wants to do the same thing," said Sarah.

"Hang up the phone, now." whispered Marie.

"I was telling her that she cannot apply unless we change this profile."

"Just tell her she was not accepted last semester, it was a mistake."

Five months ago, Sofi's father did not want her to attend Harvard. Marie is a former friend of Mr. Parker, the father of Sofi, and she is in charge of the admissions. Being at a level where she can choose who may have admission to her field or not, she receives the call from her old friend who tells her that her daughter must not be accepted at Harvard.

"Why? We already accepted her," said the lady.

"Cancel it, and I will do the rest."

"OK, can you tell me why are you doing this?"

"No, sorry."

Apparently, the director forgot to erase the traces and the assistant came over it. The excellent way to relieve stress is to do an important job by yourself and not to confide it to someone because most of the time you will be disappointed.

Being stressed out of failing to do the dirty job, Marie tells Sarah that if Sofi calls her back, she must say it was a misunderstanding. As soon as Sofi calls back, she plays the scene as she was told. Sofi is not convinced of the speech of Sarah, she calls James to explain the case. James does not delay to join Sofi.

Arriving at Sofi's dwelling house, he sits down and Sofi explains to him what happened, but what intrigued her is the way the assistant changed her mind as someone who was given orders.

"We can verify if you want," said James, "bring your laptop." James tried to hack the university network.

They spend the whole evening. He realizes that it's harder than he thought. After spending the whole day and evening without success, he proposes her another alternative which includes him going back soon to Boston before class starts.

"What kinda idea?" Sofi asks.

"I have a friend who has the key of the chest that we want to open."

"Can you speak English, please?"

"He could help me access to the school network."

The class is going to start in a few days, and James had foreseen passing by his cousin. He decides to shorten his break, so he explains to his parents without mentioning about hacking the university.

"When do you want to go?" asked Sofi.

"Tomorrow." He responds tentatively

"Please stay, we haven't spent enough time together."

"That's why I am going, it's to help us to have enough time together."

Sofi understand what's at stake, she makes it easy for him and accepts his argument.

Spending 2 days with his cousin John and his wife Jasmine and his little nephew Ryan in New York, he continues to Boston. Welcomed with overwhelming open arms from his friends. Michael and Carol enjoy life, as for Waleed, he remains the same funniest single man. James wants to talk to Michael in private.

"Can I borrow him for a moment, Carol?"

"Not for long, and I hope you did not forget that I promised to kill you when you come back, do it quick."

"OK, girl love you…"

James solicits Michael's help about the key of the university's website. Michael has already deactivated the CODE. James needs help to know if what Sofi said is true. Michael was obligated to deactivate the code because Carol goes into his room. He did not want her to know that he has a code that allows him access to the university website, so he disabled it.

"Can you activate it just for a minute?"

"OK, let me say goodbye to Carol."

At Michael's, he takes out his computer and sends his secret code. After having inserted it, he obtains the control of the site, and he asks James what he is looking for. James gives him the information.

After seeing what he is looking for, he realizes that Sofi was right, he prints the paper and puts it in his pocket as proof and leaves.

He shows it to the director in charge of the admissions. When Mary sees the paper, she flurries and says, "Where did you get that?"

"Does it matter?" said James.

"What do you want?"

"Not only will you lose your job, but you'll also go to prison. Your only way out is this will be my clemency. you accept her, and nobody is going to know about this."

"I can't."

"Why?" he asked.

She explains that she does not know why, but the father of Sofi is behind it, and he is someone who he would not like to mess up with.

"I know him; he is the director of the CIA. And you are the director here, so he is not your boss," James said.

Seeing the cold hard stare from the face of James, she realizes that she does not have a choice, so she takes the risk of accepting his proposal. "You know what you're right, he is not my boss."

"Smart after all." James walks out of the office like nothing happened.

Chapter 14

The Hackers

Using the code was not the best idea but it was the only option for James to get what he wants. After finishing with the code, they forgot to deactivate it. Remembering an hour later, Michael goes to deactivate it in a hurry before it falls into bad hands. He disables the code without noticing that hackers have modified it remotely. Those hackers have used the breach to infiltrate the network of the website which allows them to access other highly secure institutions. Catastrophe caused by the modification of the algorithms James did by using the code that they found on Steve's computer.

The NASA notices that one of their satellites has been hacked, and before they try to figure out how it happened, they catch sight of some flying objects on their screen coming towards Planet Earth. They have the protocol of not to panic in this kind of situation, otherwise they will not be able to find a solution. As the objects approaches, the NASA agents realize that they are saucers. The NASA let the NSA know that they have been hacked, and flying objects have direction down to Earth, and some clarifications about the hack will be necessary.

A whole week the UFOs are wandering on the sky under the eyes of authorities acting like nothing is happening as always. Poor population is not aware of what is happening. The hackers need to have as much control as possible before they embark on their Machiavellian plan and the government thinks that it is better if those UFO remain unknowing from the population for national security matters.

Mr. Parker receives a call from her daughter, at the end of the call he hangs up unhappy and disappointed. He summons Marie at his office, but she already knows what it is about. She retorts, "You can't summon me, you're not my boss."

"Why do I receive the news that my daughter is going to Harvard?" he asked, "I believed in you, you told me that you'll handle it," retorted Mr. Parker.

She does not hesitate in telling him that she has been forced to accept Sofi under the threat of losing her job. Mr. Parker laughs, and asks her if it never crossed her mind that he cannot make her lose her pathetic job that she likes so much.

Mrs. Marie swallows hard and becomes silent for a moment, "I don't know why are you doing this."

"None of your business, just fix it."

"You can ask me a favor, but you cannot give me the order to do something for you that we all know is against the law."

"OK, I'm asking you a favor."

Mrs. Marie is trying to make him understand that her hands are tied. In any case, it's too late, and if she tries to stop her, they both will deal with the consequences.

"First it's your daughter, you don't want her to know, and second, I have this conversation on tape," said Marie.

"Are you threatening me now?" said Mr. Parker.

"No, I'm telling you to back off like a longtime friend."

Angry, Mr. Parker hangs up the phone and throws it away.

Meanwhile, Sofi is ready to make her dream come true, going to Harvard and above all, to stay close to the love of her life. While waiting for Sofi at the airport with his friends, James seems nervous as if it is his first time to meet with Sofi.

"Relax man," said Carol.

"I'm trying, perhaps it's because I am so excited to see her talking to me after all we've been through," said James.

Every girl who shows up at the exit, his friends ask him if it is her, after spending half an hour waiting, they are tired of wasting saliva asking if it is her. Suddenly, a different girl appears, "If it's like you told me, she's here honey."

"I thought I've already told you not to call me honey, or I'll tell everybody about anppiotment, no, no...wait, artichecture you prefer that, right!" said James.

"Fine," snapped Waleed.

"What did I tell you?" asked James.

"You told me that Sofi makes you forget Rawan, and I see only one here who could do that."

"Hum?"

"She is coming right there."

James runs to hug her and squeezes her tight in his arms, lift her up and rotates. She is as happy as James. James introduces his friends to Sofi and

Carol says, "Wow, looks like someone knows how to pick his prey, ooh!" She puts her hands in her mouth to stop the sentence from getting out but too late.

Sofi raises her head, looks at James and says, "What prey?"

"Yes, what prey Carol?" asked James to Carol earnestly.

Carol feels embarrassed. "Relax." James says to Carol, he had already told her about Rawan, she does not have to feel guilty.

"Ohh gosh, this is really embarrassing" said Carol.

"Yeah, it is, this is what happens when people can't keep their mouth shut." said Michael.

Carol smiles and hides behind Michael in embarrassment.

"You wanna eat something first before we go home?" said Waleed to Sofi.

They all yell at Waleed, "Nooooooo...you just ate."

"Whatever," said Waleed peevishly.

The friends get into the car and head to the campus, to show her around, as classes start the next day. After a very long day, Sofi unpacks her luggage at James' apartment, and she calls her mother to let her know that she has landed, and she hopes it will be a wonderful semester. In ongoing conversation, her phone switches off abruptly. She throws the phone on the bed and keeps working. James calls her from his room and asks if she has network, his phone is not working.

"Sorry, mine is dead too," she answered.

Sofi heads to the bathroom for a hot bath while James is making a sandwich. Suddenly, he spots on the laptop that Michael entrusted him when they activated the code open in front of him making some weird writings running at full speed. He runs towards it to have a look, but it is too late, the computer is off. He sits there, anxiously. Knowing that it is not a good sign, he goes looking for his phone to call Michael. Unfortunately, he still does not have a network, but he has the Wi-Fi of the university that is making signals on his phone. When he goes to his room to take the flash drive that contains all his files, he sees bright lights that clears his room; he looks through the window and sees a big engine that he had seen just on movies.

Having waited for the device to lie down, he guesses that it is an UFO, and from it he sees creatures getting out. Indescribable creatures, and they all look alike moving towards his house. Panicked he cannot figure out what to do, he heads into the bathroom, finds Sofi who is about to open her mouth, he covers it before she makes a noise. After having cut off the water and turning off the light, he mouths to Sofi that there is something in the house. Hearing their noises and their unknown language, he realizes that they are not just creatures, but creatures from another planet, armed with weapons made by advanced level of intelligence. After going through the house without finding anything, the unwanted guests turn around and climb into the UFO and leaves.

"What game was that James, is it hallowing yet?" groaned Sofi.

"I wish it was a game," said James.

James tries to warn Michael, but he does not have network. He grabs the hand of Sofi and runs to the exit; he enters the car and starts the engine. They go to Michael, speeding as fast as they can. Once at Michael, they bang the door, yelling at him to open, looking around the area like an afraid chicken.

"What took you so long?" said James and pushes the door.

"I was in bed dude, don't you two sleep?"

"We don't have time, follow us now, I'll explain to you later."

Michael wants to know what happens before he moves, but James doesn't give him the choice. Wanting to get out of the house Sofi sees their companions heading towards their second target's house, Michael. She warns James and Michael that they have companions.

"Who are they?" Michael asks and Sofi let him see through the window.

"How about this for some explanations?" asked James.

"How do we get out of here," said Michael with fear in his voice after having the slightest glimpse of them.

"Man, for that we need the car, and you see they are waiting at the car," said Sofi.

"OK come with me, this way, I am the only one who knows it," said Michael.

They follow him and find themselves in a place outside the enclosure of the aliens, nearby, there is a bar they enter. Michael begins to ask questions, and James tells him what he saw happening in front of his eyes with the laptop, and sometime later, the creatures show up.

Sitting in the bar waiting to see if they are going to be left alone, they see on the news that an American missile has reached a communication satellite of Russia. Before they have time to get out of the bar after breathing a shot, another news come out again, a Russian missile hits an American aircraft carrier. While everybody in the bar is in shock trying to get out of there, the three others are petrified knowing that they are being haunted for God knows why.

"Please tell me this is a bad dream, please," said James.

"Why is all of this happening?" said Sofi.

"No, why are those ugly and strange creatures trying to kill us," snapped Michael.

Michael remembers that James talked about the problem of the computer and that the creatures came at his house a moment later. James looks at Michael, lost in his imagination and asks him what he is thinking about.

"What if Steve's death was not an accident," said Michael.

"What are you talking about?" asked James.

"When he took the code, and he knew what it is for, he died. We used the same code to activate the site weeks ago, and we forgot to deactivate it," said Michael.

"You are delusional, come on man," said Sofi.

"I think he might be right, I have already seen this code before, I wanted to tell you but I didn't have the answers you'd have asked," claims James.

"Where did you see it?" asked Mike.

"In my dad's stuff."

Sofi looks at James in the eyes and asks him which biological or adoptive.
"Please don't start this at this moment of misery." Begged James

"No, the question is why are they after us? What have this code triggered?"

"If…if my father was right! We're being invaded by aliens, and we're the ones that opened the door for them which makes us their vulnerability." Said James chokingly as he looks at Sofi.

"I wasn't going to judge. My mother told me. I know you were right about everything."

"Really?" asked James.

"Why do you think I forgave you after you left without saying goodbye? Because I'm just nice! Nope I'm not that nice."

"Wait! By Aliens you mean extraterrestrial creatures, not as these people out of the country coming here?" Asked Michael, and James nods

Michael looks out the window, it's quiet outside. Wanting to take a step outside, he sees several shining eyes. He runs back, they arrive in the bar, everyone is scared the manager of the bar turns the TV off.

"Who is there?" he asked

"I don't know! why don't you go check?" said Michael.

Afraid without knowing what is going on, the consumers jostle on leaving the bar, and someone drop his cellphone and James snatches it and puts it in his pocket. They seize the opportunity to infiltrate the crowd and go out without being apprehended by the aliens. After leaving the bar, they rush at James's house.

Both governments are asking questions about those fired missiles that they don't know anything about. Given that it is a war declaration, the presidents of the two countries want to respond, but their ministers and secretaries prevent them from reacting before knowing what is really happening. The Russian president receives a call from the American president asking him what happened and the other asks the same question. Each one does not believe the other's sayings, so they try to see clearly in the situation.

Chapter 15

The Fugitives

NSA analysts begin looking for the cause. Following a large number of attempts, they realize that the computer is not theirs, but a computer located in the US territory has sent the two missiles. After having localized the computer, they inform the FBI, which visit James. At their arrival at James', they knock at the door. While James is searching for his flash drive in the room with Sofi, Michael is in the living room, he hears two human voices, and he opens the door.

"Wow, thank God," raps out Michael.

"FBI, we are going to ask you to follow us," said one of the agents.

"Why, what did I do?"

"No more questions. Where is your computer?"

James and Sofi hear the agents talking with Michael. James wants to get out of the room, Sofi grabs him by the hand and says, "Where are you going? They're going to arrest you before you say anything, stay here."

The agents begin to search for the computer after Michael refused to talk. Michael realizes that if they go into the room they'll find James, so he gets softened, bows down to take the computer, and he make a sign to James and Sofi, hiding in the closet, not to move. The agents take the computer, and Michael with them. On their way out of the apartment, there are two aliens waiting.

"What the hell?" said one of the agents.

"I think we are dead now, and that will be your fault," said Michael.

The aliens start shooting at them with alien weapons, whose bullets could pass through any non-solid barrier. The officers try to protect themselves by shooting back but realize that their bullets have no effect on the aliens. James and Sofi are watching the scene through the window. One of the officers arrives to open the door of the car and starts it while the other got shot in her leg. Michael is on cuffs, but he manages to drag her out of sight. She gives him the manacle's keys. Michael removes them and helps her to get to the car while the other covers them. Michael and the wounded agent crawl on the ground until they get to the car and leave.

"What was that?" asked the woman.

"I do not know but I think they are here for me and…"

"And who?"

"And you I guess," said Michael.

The aliens follow the car with their strange machine without knowing that James and Sofi are in the house. James takes the flash drive, his father's files, and his code book, and proposes Sofi to go and stay with Carol since she is not concerned.

"How can you say that? We are in this together, I am not leaving."

"Fine, come. I have to call Carol and Waleed to tell them not to try to contact us," said James.

"OK, let me call my dad. Maybe he could help."

"No, the last time my dad called a government agent, he and my mom disappeared. I'm not doing the same mistake," said James.

"Do you think the same story is taking place?" said Sofi.

She sees a fear in James's eyes that she had never seen before.

"Maybe, I don't know," he said. He takes the phone he stole at the bar, and calls Carol and Waleed and tells them not to try to contact him or contact Michael otherwise they would be in danger.

"Did you watch the news four hours ago?" said Carol.

"About what?" asked James.

"The missiles."

"I think it has something to do with us, Michael and I that is why I told you to switch off your phone and do not talk to anyone."

After losing the track of Michael and the FBI agents, the aliens turn to launch the following procedure. In the interrogation room, Michael tries to make the interrogators understand that he is innocent; his computer has been hacked. While sitting in the interrogation room, Michael sees all the officers running in the same direction. His interrogator named Raymond Culture, the best agent on the field, goes out and sees everyone heads up on the main screen of the office watching the latest news that just surfaced on all the channels, and that is more frightening than the first two. The aliens pass a message saying they have control of air and road traffic and they are going to have the control of the communication satellites soon. They give an ultimatum of 7 hours to the government to deliver Michael to them. Culture returns to the interrogation room and shows the video to Michael.

"These creatures I've seen are able to do more than this," said Michael with a big fear.

"Why do they want you?"

"I don't think that they're talking about me," said Michael.

Having seen the information on TV like everybody, Sofi gets frightened, she cannot stand not knowing what's wrong, so she asks James what happens.

"I know it sounds crazy, but you have to trust me."

"What? You can't tell, right?" asked Sofi angrily.

"No, someone hacked a computer that was in my possession, and the computer had apparently something very important on it," said James.

"So why did you not get rid of the computer."

"It's not this one, it's Michael's friend's computer, and the FBI agents took it with them when they took Michael."

"Do you know why they want Michael?" asked Sofi.

"How am I supposed to know that?" asked James.

James does not say to Sofi that this is the code they used to hack the admission office that is at the origin of all this.

At the meantime, Michael does not want to answer the FBI agent who loses his patience and begins to move to the top level of the interrogation. He intends to have answers by any means necessary. Suddenly, he receives the call from his superior who tells him that the CIA wants the boy. Michael realizes that it is getting serious.

When they come for Michael, "Is it really necessary that I follow them?" asked Michael to special agent Culture.

"Yeah, and I think you're going to have fun there," said Culture to Michael.

The CIA takes Michael into the Pentagon. Arrived at the Pentagon, Michael receives the visit of someone accompanied by several bodyguards, "Wha, what, what is this?" groped Michael.

"This is your nightmare son, and I'm really sorry for what's about to happen," said Culture.

Michael watches him get out of the room while the other arrives.

"Who are you? I told them about the whole thing that I pretend to know."

"Oh, really what did you tell them, could you tell me if you don't mind? By the way, I'm the director." Michael does not understand what's going on, the agent frightened him saying that this director is going to be his worst nightmare, and he finds out that the director wants to have a civilized discussion. Michael says he knows nothing else after telling him what he told the FBI.

"Who owns this computer if you don't know anything," asked the director.

"The computer belonged to my friend who died in a car accident, and I wanted to know more about his death then as the accident was bound to this computer, I kept it," said Michael.

"In your opinion, who the hacker could be?"

"I do not know. I was not there."

"Who was there?" Michael refuses to answer. The director asks for a second time, and Michael still refuses to answer.

"I don't think it's necessary for me to remind you what's going to happen in 7hrs if we don't deliver you to those people. No, wait I was going to say in 5hrs now if you don't answer me. Would you have the blood of all these people in your hands! Is that what you want?" asked the director angrily.

"Who told you those are people? They are not humans," asked Michael.

The director takes the chair and sits with his mouth open for a long time and said, "Nothing can make a message on all the chains of the world besides humans, or, or something more intelligent and advanced than the humans."

"The FBI agents did not tell you anything, did he?" asked Michael.

"They are in the hospital after the ambush, they are in shock."

"These are aliens, not humans."

The director thinks that Michael is abusing of his patience, so he threatens him to put him in detention. Michael begs him to go ask the FBI agents in the hospital. He leaves the room running to seek confirmation of the FBI agents arriving at the hospital; he finds the agent injured in her leg is dead because of a deadly poison contained in the bullet. The agent number two cannot speak until the director says the word aliens, he raises his head, looks at him and begins nodding his head vigorously. The director returns to his headquarters.

James and Sofi are on the look-out for a quiet place to take refuge until they find a solution. Being in a hotel that they have the chance to find in the middle of the night, they do not sleep, they stay in the living room checking out every minute. James takes out his computer to see what he can do; Sofi catches his hand and advises him not to do it. He puts the computer away and goes to sit next to Sofi. Alone in the area with a dead silence, Sofi leans her head on James' shoulder, "Do you ever think about the future?" pouted Sofi.

"Yeah, I used to," answered James.

"You used to huh?"

"Yeah, I used to think about you and me living the rest of our life together."

Sofi looks at him and says, "Really? What about now?"

"I found out that it was just adolescent's dream. You know since you did not believe me when I told you I can't talk about my family, and you hated me that I was protecting you. That made me think a lot. I realize that thinking about the future is destroying your life because you don't know if it is going to happen. Now I would like to live without knowing what is going to happen tomorrow or after tomorrow, I want to live the present moment and let the future decide what it has for me, but I do know one thing, I will always love you," said James.

Sofi falls asleep on James's shoulder. Suddenly, James receives the call from his adoptive parents; he does not wait to answer and asks if they are fine.

"Yes, yes, we are. Are you?" said the father.

"Why are you calling me at this hour?" said James.

"You to tell us, our son is at a university with a friend who is claimed by people want to make the apocalypse."

"What are you talking about?" said James.

"Do not play with me son," said Mr. Barry, "I told you I will always be there for you, I know all your friends and what you are doing so tell me what's going on?"

James starts explaining his terrible evening since he went to the airport to pick up Sofi until this present moment, and he does not know why they want Michael. Mr. Barry tells him not to try to contact Michael, it's not Michael they want it's him. James asks how does he know that.

"Why do you think your dad and your mom sacrifice themselves for you? You are special, you have something they need, and they want you," said Mr. Barry.

"How do you know that Dad?"

"Your dad was preventing that when he disappeared."

Mr. Barry tells James not to get caught in any way; otherwise, he will put the world at risk.

The director turns to the interrogation room to ask questions to Michael, but this time he is determined to use a rather unconventional way to make Michael talk. Arriving in the room, he starts by clearing the table and throwing the chair on the other side, he takes off his suit to cover the camera. Michael lectures him about the constitution saying that these acts are prohibited by the law and that he has no right to torture him.

"Watch me," answered the director.

"I am a US citizen, you cannot do this" said Michael with a fear.

"The Pentagon is independent, we do not follow any law, and here you're not in the US territory, so you have 59 seconds, starting now," said the director.

Michael resist until the minute finishes, he sees machines getting into the room.

"I'll talk, his name is James, he was there, the computer was in his apartment."

"So easy, wasn't it?" said the director.

The director gets out of the room and gives the order to all departments to do research on every James; Michael has been in contact with. Time is about to finish, the authorities do not want to give Michael to the aliens before knowing how he would be useful to them. Another message appears on the screens saying that the ultimatum is about to end by specifying that there are only 30 minutes remaining and that no one will be able to prevent what is going to happen after these 30 minutes. The directors of the major institutions are summoned to the crisis room by the president. There are only about 20 minutes left and they still do not know what it is. The president says, "What's the problem besides what this kid told us about aliens. What do they want from him? Find everything about him because to find a solution to something there must be a problem, isn't it?"

"Yes, Mr. President, I think we have no choice but to believe the kid and hand him to them," said one of the president secretaries.

"Are you insane? He's just a kid and we don't know what they're going to do to him," said the president. While they are in the middle of a conference, a secretary at the White House opens the door.

"Excuse me, I think you'd like to see this." She turns on the TV. They see car accidents in some major city of the world caused by the hack of the traffic lights which causes the death of several people. Another message is sent that informs them they have another hour to avoid planes to fall down tragically from the sky like birds. Now that all governments are concerned, they call the US to find out more about the cause, unfortunately, even the US does not have the answer.

"Mr. President, would you please consider my thought to give them the kid," said the secretary.

"I want to talk to him," said the president.

The director of the CIA goes in person, seeks Michael. Before handing Michael over to the president, he whispered to him one last thing.

At the briefing room, the president asks him if he has any idea what the aliens want.

"No, I don't Mr. President," said Michael.

Alone with Michael in an office, isolated, the president shows Michael what happened in the last hour when he was in detention. The video shocks Michael and he asks the president what he can do to avoid the worst. The president appreciates his courage, but let him know that he is not obligated to do anything if he does not want to.

"What's going to happen to me is not important compared to what's happening now, we do not have time and a choice," said Michael.

The president looks at Michael and wants to impede him from doing so, but he cannot because they are out of time and there's no other alternatives.

The president asks Michael if he has the last wish that he would like the president to do for him before he goes.

"Yes, mister president, I would like you to tell my parents that I am sorry, and tell my girlfriend, Carol, I love her."

"I'll son and I'm really sorry," said the president with compassion.

Less than 30 minutes before the time flow, the aliens send another message that says, "You made the right choice."

"How did they know that we have decided to give them Michael?" asked the president to his directors and secretaries.

There is no need for response from secretaries or directors. The aliens post a message, "We have access to all surveillance cameras, and if you try to disable one of them you would suffer the consequences." The president orders the officer to give Michael to the aliens.

Chapter 16

The Escape

The agents, charged to deliver Michael, arrive at the planned location. The agents have the orders to leave Michael at the rendezvous and go. They leave Michael in the middle of nowhere, a very vast and deserted area. Michael is there as someone for his death sentence hoping that his death will be quick and painless. While standing there, imagining all possible ways he could be decapitated. As soon as he is in the hands of the aliens, an immense UFO approaches slowly above his head. When it lands, two aliens come out, ugly, nastier and scarier than what he saw before. Their physical appearances make him swoon; the aliens take him into their locomotive.

The president of the free world, very concerned about the future of his reign, receives calls from all the others great countries president. Afraid of what is about to happen after the aliens have received the young man who allowed them to penetrate into all the computer's networks. They reproach him for not being able to secure his network, and that they will take him responsible for everything that is going to happen in the future if there is one. The president tries to convince them not to panic and to stay positive. Little he knows about someone's dignity. There are two major things that can show the true face of dignity, hunger and fear.

While Michael is napping after passing out, James and Sofi are on the run, the authorities are counting the humans and materials losses they have sustained from the accidents. Some people leave the big cities for the countryside, knowing that it is only the beginning of a long catastrophe.

Michael's sleep was long; finally, he wakes up in a bed without remembering what really happened. How he got there. He gets up and looks around for someone to explain to him what happened. When he leaves the room that he had never seen before by its splendor, he sees an alien with an automatic weapon in his hand. Suddenly, the memory returns to him, the alien beckons him to return to his room. A moment later, another alien comes to visit him in his room.

"Hello!" said the alien.

"Wha…t! This is ridiculous," said Michael.

Michael wonders how a creature like this can speak English.

"What is ridiculous, is it my physical appearance? I can change that."

The alien becomes a real human, "No way! How do you do that?"

The alien changes himself to become Michael. Michael looks at him, "Oh! Cool, you're shapeshifters too. It's like I'm in front of a mirror, wow, that's impressive." Michael already forgot the purpose of his presence in the UFO until the weapon pointed to him reminds him.

He starts worrying about, what is following next. "Where did you learn how to speak my language?" asked Michael to the alien.

"Here," he answered. "What do you want from me? If you want to kill me; do it because I am not gonna snitch on anyone or do anything to help you," cried Michael.

"Why are you crying? You are not going to suffer to death, not if you tell me what I want to know."

"Never!" retorted Michael.

"OK, I'll ask you the question. Where is James and the computer?"

"Oh that's it! James? Why do you want him?"

"None of your business."

Michael refuses to respond to the alien. The alien goes out of the room and returns a few minutes later accompanied by two other aliens more frightening with torture machines. He finds out that it is more serious than he thought. "Come on not again!" he whimpered

"Are you going to tell me what I asked you?" said the alien.

"Why do you want James?"

"One, he has something that I need, and second, I have something for him."

"If I don't, what are you going to do?"

"You'll endure the most painful torture you've never seen even in horror movies until you beg me to kill you, and I'll use all of the power I have to destroy everybody who has the woe to meet you, even all your friends in Facebook, snapchat, Instagram all that shit." snapped the alien to Michael.

Michael manages to find out what they are going to do with the computer or James, but the alien says nothing. Michael is never going to let something happen to his friends, but he does not know where James is.

"I don't know where he is," he said weakly.

"I know, but you have his phone number, right?"

"Yeah, but he is not crazy to let his phone on, or carry it with him."

"Just tell me the number, and you are free, this has nothing to do with you."

Michael gives him the number of James, knowing that he got rid of it.

After receiving the number of James, the alien goes in the main room to localize, but he knows that James is not so naive to let his phone turned on while he is the most wanted. The aliens acquire all the data of his phone, all his contacts and all the last activities that he realized with his phone. They get the number of Sofi and localize it without difficulty. James adoptive father contrived to hack Sofi's phone the first day she went at their house with James. Now it is a good use to him. While keeping eyes on James by tracking the phone of Sofi, he realizes that someone else is hacking the phone to be able to track it. James's father calls on Sofi's phone and warns him that they will receive a visit in a few moments, they must leave the hotel.

"How do you know that?"

"They're looking for you now," said Mr. Barry.

James put the flash drive in his sock and hides the computer in a place in the room. He wakes Sofi up in hurry, wanting to return to see if they have company, he finds Mr. Parker at the door with three other agents who drugs him with a sedative and take him with them. Being in the room, Sofi talks to James and receives no answer, she leaves the room no sight of James, she finds the door open looks outside and she sees a big black SUV moving away, she begins to panic. Wishing to get out of the room and go to join Carol and Waleed, because they are the only friends she knows where to find, the UFO of the aliens' lands and some aliens come to take her terrified by the creatures she begins to scream and to fight, but it does not help her. They take her by force, and throw her in their UFO because of her annoying screams. The aliens let Michael hang around their shuttle after cooperating. He tries to go into the main room of the UFO, he sees doppelgangers everywhere, and most of all good looking and robust humans, but as he approaches them, he realizes that they are not humans they are more giant and beautiful and the hair is long white in color like elves, and they communicate with each other by a language that he had never heard before. At the next door, he sees technologies that he could qualify 100 years ahead of human technology. He approaches the main screen and sees that the aliens have an eye on everything that they want to see around the world.

Some moment after he sees Sofi escorted by aliens, he runs towards her and asks her where James is.

"I don't know, he woke me up in hurry, and when I woke up, he was gone," said Sofi.

"Where?" asked Michael.

"I don't know," she said with panic, "but I saw a car drive away, I think someone took him. What are you doing here by the way, I thought you were dead when they caught you?" muttered Sofi.

"I'm not dead for now, they were trying to locate you by taking me, they never needed me."

"We have to escape, we are in danger here, and what are these creatures, some are terrifying, some are strange, and some are perfect," hissed Sofi to Michael.

"Yeah we have to go find James before them."

Planning to escape from someone who has eyes on the sky good luck with that. Soon, a perfect time presents itself; while the aliens are busy looking for a way to find James. They take the opportunity to get out without being apprehended. Viewing that the UFO is on the ground, it would make thing less hard. Once outside they do not know that the aliens have let them out of full bloom because they already have part of what they need to start their chaos. Michael and Sofi begin to run without stopping until they leave the hostile environment.

When they were at the hotel for James, the aliens took the computer that James concealed without Sofi noticing.

"Didn't you find it easy?" asked Michael.

"What?" ask Sofi.

"Our escape, with all this technology and that open door we've found."

"Yes, I think they have something else, they wouldn't have let us leave so easily."

"So what are we going to do now?"

"I do not know maybe we can go see my father, he is an agent of the government, he can help us."

"OK!"

Michael demands about her phone to make the call. Unfortunately, she left it at the hotel when she was taken, "Wait; wait…I got it, my phone was turned on that's why they located us." All of the sudden the thoughts of what James was talking about her father come to her mind.

"And?"

"I think I know who kidnapped James," said Sofi.

"Who?"

"My father, he localized my phone because he knew I was with James. And the car I saw was the government's car," said Sofi.

"We will have a look at your father afterwards, but first of, I would like to see if Carol is doing well, and I have to talk to the president," said Michael.

"I think my father could help with that, I have an emergency number on which I can call him at any time." They go into a telephone booth and Sofi tells him the number.

"Hi Dad, it's me, Sofi."

"Where are you, sweetheart? I am coming to pick you up," said Mr. Parker. "Is James with you?"

"No, why would he be?" the father played innocent.

"Someone kidnapped him. Is Mom OK?" cried Sofi.

"Yeah she is fine, she is scared, but she is fine, she is going to be here soon."

Sofi requires her father to help her get in contact with the president, and it is very important. Mr. Parker becomes suspicious, who that can be since she is not with James. When he asks to know about him, she says that his name is Michael.

"How do you know him?" Mr. Parker asked.

He wants to know if this is the Michael he had in detention.

"He's a friend of James and mine," she answered.

"Can I talk to him?"

Michael takes the phone, and he asks if he can talk to the president.

"Did they let you go?"

"Do I know you?" asked Michael.

"I don't think so, but I know you were given to the alien, I am working for the government."

Michael covers the microphone of the phone and asks Sofi if it is her father, because the ton sounds familiar.

"Yeah, it is my dad."

"Can we trust him? Because there are some people in the government that I do not trust."

"Are you serious? I said it's my dad." She snapped

"OK."

Michael tells him that he escaped and his escape was too easy to be one, so he is sure that they have something that will allow them to reach their goal. Michael adds that they must disable any electronic weapon.

"What's about to start," asked Mr. Parker.

"The apocalypse," said Michael.

Michael hangs up the phone in hope that the president will get the message. Sofi suggests to Michael that they go to the hotel room to see if they could have clues that will help them know why the aliens let them go, and why James was kidnapped. Michael is sure the aliens have James, because they never needed him, it was only a way of camouflaging their true intention, and he is sure that the end of the planet is coming because the aliens are advanced in technology that humans will not reach in a hundred years. No government has an evolving technology that rivals theirs.

James regains consciousness and sees in front of him two people with Mr. Parker in a strange repository. James asks Mr. Parker what he is doing there instead of doing his job when the nation needs him the most.

"I'm doing my job right now," said Mr. Parker.

"Does your job include holding me hostage and drugging me?"

"Yes, we are going to change the world in 30 minutes, the rest of the UFOs will begin to land in all 4 corners around the world and it will be without pity, believe me," said Mr. Parker.

James tied up in the chair can barely move; raises his head slowly thinking that he is hallucinating, thinking that he did not hear what he just heard. He looks at Mr. Parker.

"Please, don't tell me that you have anything to do with this sir."

"Why not, I have waited for this long time, and here we are."

Being aware that the aliens have what they need to carry out their mission Mr. Parker injects James another sedative to put him out of condition to harm. The director is ready for anything to prevent him from getting his nose in his business.

More UFOs are beginning to be detected by radars. The US president summons the heads of all the US army and advises the same to other presidents, a moment later he makes a press conference to reassure his citizens that they will fight all together until their last blow if necessary.

The press conference made by the US president had an impact reaction on all governments around the world. First in the US there are bunch of pissed off rednecks that decide if the aliens are going to take over the Earth they will have to pass over their body. Every country combines forces to fight the enemy, even governments that don't like each other. The president of North Korea suggests to the President of China and South Korea to join their resources together to protect their population and their continent. The president of Russia convinces the UK's queen and all other countries in Europe to be one, it might help them to be stronger than the aliens, which all countries agree. The Middle East is trying to be on the same page, for the first time in history. Palestine and Israel have the same concerns other than to kill or threaten each other. Saudi Arabia is worried if the USA can help them in this case, so Iran and Iraq bring some of their soldiers in Saudi Arabia to help them. For the first time African's presidents think about people who they are in charge of and not about only themselves. The leaders of all kind of terrorists find out that they have now the real jihad that they have to face instead of killing innocent people, claiming that they are doing it for a religion, so they join their army to participate in the war. Great leaders around the world are willing to do their best to save the world, and stop thinking about self-interest. All countries recruit brave people who are able to help in any ways like pilots, drivers and shooters.

Michael and Sofi go seeking refuge at Carol's house. Carol's father is a war veteran who is retired, and he has his proper business with Carol's mother. Carol's father is a paranoid man who always told himself this days would arrive only he did not know when, so he made himself a bunker while he was still a soldier. This bunker has a width that can contain more than 20 people with a food ration that can hold a maximum of 3 months. After seeing what was going on over the whole evening, Harry, Carol's father, prepared the place for his family and neighbors.

Chapter 17
James' Nightmare

When they arrive at Carol's, Michael and Sofi knock on the door and no one answers. Michael goes around the house to see if he could see anything, screaming, "Carol…Caroline, where are you?"

Already in the bunker, they can hear an undistinctive voice, but Carol recognizes the voice. She rushes to get out, but her father caught her, she struggles, he refuses to let her go, "It's Michael, please Michael is there open for him, please" She cried.

Harry tells everyone to step back, and he holds his gun with one hand and opens the door with the other. Once in, Michael runs into Carol's arms. "Happy to see you again," said Sofi to Waleed, and Carol sheds tears in Michael shoulder, "What happened, I was so worried."

Waleed comes to hug Sofi and said, "Where is James?"

"I don't know who kidnaped him," Sofi explained to Waleed and Carol what happened to her and Michael and James since they went home, and why they did not call them.

"Where is he now?" asked Waleed.

"I thought that my dad kidnaped him, but he said he did not when we called him," said Sofi.

"What made you think he did that?" asked Harry.

"He was the only one who has my number; I think he tracked my phone that is why they found us."

"How the aliens had your number?" asked Harry to Sofi, and Michael raises his hand and answers, "That'd be me. I was obligated to give it to them, they were threatening to kill all of you. They control all of our satellites."

"Do you know where your father is?" said Harry.

"No."

Harry goes back to the bunker, and takes a briefcase, which contains a computer that can help him locate a phone call.

"What are you doing Harry?" said Carol's mother.

"I want to help her find her dad and friend, call him," said Harry to Sofi.

"I don't have my phone."

Harry gives her his phone to call her father, and as Harry confirmed, her father won't tell her where he is, so she must make the conversation last.

"Hi, Dad!"

"Hi, honey! What's up?"

"I did not find James."

"Oh, really!"

Sofi makes the conversation go on as Harry asked. When the phone is located to a place unworthy of a high-ranking government agent, Harry becomes leery, but does not say anything to her. Sofi sees the truth in his eyes and asks him the address. He writes the address on a piece of paper and puts it in his pocket. She extends her hand.

"Are you out of your mind? Where do you wanna go?" asked Waleed and Michael.

"I'm not letting him down, do not even try to stop me. He's the only hope this planet has." She cried.

"I'll go," asked Michael.

After a long discussion about who is going or staying. Harry checks if his gun has enough bullets and says, "Nobody is going; I am the only one who is going."

Discussing who is going and who is not, they hear a loud noise echoing outside, everybody shut their mouth. Sofi pulls the sheet out of Harry's pocket and runs to the door, opens it; he catches her and she begs him to let her go. He accepts on the condition that they go together; Michael and Waleed refuse to stay while their best friend is missing.

At four, they go to the located place. Exiting the bunker, they see lights illuminated by dozens of UFOs a few kilometers of height and waiting for the right moment to land. They close the door behind them. At the entrance of the warehouse, Sofi recognizes the corpse of the two agents lying down. They were present with her father at her graduation day. They continue walking slowly, paying attention with their eyes and ears open.

James wakes up again and begins again the questions.

"Oh man, seriously can't you sleep? You are so annoying," asked Mr. Parker.

"Why are you doing this, don't you care about your family?" asked James.

"I'm doing this for them and for people in the world, and I'll be the king of the world."

"This is ridiculous, do you think they are going to let you do it, no, they are going to kill you after having what they need."

"Shut up, you are like your father?" rapped out Mr. Parker.

"What?"

"Your dad had the ability to be in my place 15 years ago, he did not take the chance, now it is my turn."

"How do you know my father?"

"I was the one who he came to see when he discovered it, and he warned me that the world was going to be invaded. I told him what to do, he ignored it, and he tried to run, I caught him with your mother…"

"And?"

"I killed them."

James start crying, "Why are you telling me this?" he said sobbingly.

"Because you are going to be the next in a few minutes."

"Are you really going to kill all these people just to be the king of the world?" asked James.

"Duh! If it is necessary."

"Then, who are you going to govern when all are dead including Sabrina and Sofi?"

The director remains silent, and James continues to lecture him on the good he can do if he releases him and helps him stop this disaster.

"No, it is too late," said Mr. Parker.

"Let me tell you something, I know that you asked Mrs. Mary, your old friend, to not allow Sofi to get into Harvard, and I did not say anything to her because she loves you, and I do not want to see her disappointed."

Mr. Parker receives a message on his phone asking if he has the kid, and he replies that he does. After receiving the message in their turn, the aliens know that there is nothing that could put sticks in the wheels.

Having heard and seen the face of the director, Michael remembers him, and he asks Sofi if it's her father. Sofi nods her head, disappointed and ashamed.

"You see, I told you I know this voice, and I do not trust the man behind it. You should've believed me, are you happy now?" said Michael.

"Dude no need to rub it in now, she just found out that her dad is the villain," said Waleed

Sofi looks at him scowling, and snapped, "Yes I'm overjoyed, and how do you want me to know that he is the bad guy."

"Now I presume he did not tell the president what I told him."

Surprisingly, she asks him how he knew that her father is the villain. Michael tells her what he whispered to him before he takes him to the aliens.

Having all the control of communication satellites, the aliens leave the privilege to humans to be in contact to know that the scourge touches the whole world. Untouched places have the chance to see the disasters happening in big cities like Berlin, New York, Moscow, Pyongyang, Paris, Egypt, Dubai, Hong Kong and many others. All the cities are invaded. The aliens are beginning to destroy infrastructures and massacre the people circulating on the streets.

After hours of destruction and massacre of soldiers deployed in each place of battle, everything becomes calm and the UFOs land and makes the discharges of the abominable monster without pity. The unlucky survivors in their paths are all apprehended and transported and detained as prisoners, those who resist are tortured to death.

The aliens go to presidential palaces to take control, killing some very important people of governments. They take the leadership of several countries by capturing presidents and their staff just a few hours after landing. The other governments are wondering how much time they have left to be ejected from their offices, the only place where they raise only a little finger so that their wishes are fulfilled.

The aliens connect themselves in all microphones and large digital screens, that are on the large buildings of each city to convey a message that will allow the world to have a second thought about their governments and to know the intention of their new leaders because Earth is conquered by the aliens. As Africa was conquered by Europeans. The message sent by the aliens says, "We know that you are afraid of this great change that is about to happen, but it has to happen because you are the worst creatures that the creator has brought down to Earth. Now you have new leaders, your leaders do not care about you. They only think of themselves and their families, and we do not blame them for that since most of the time the rulers of a country are the reflection of the people whom they govern. In your opinion, where are they right now? In their bunkers secured by soldiers while you die here trying to defend yourself against us."

Having heard what Mr. Parker has said to James in their hiding place, Sofi and the others expect him to leave James alone, so they can free him. Mr. Parker receives a call from the president who asks him where is he. Mr. Parker cannot have a solid alibi, so he improvises saying that he was on a track.

"Did you find anything?" asked the president.

The director of the CIA better have a valid justification for his absence, without any thought he answers, "Yes."

"What?" asked the president.

"I have the kid who programmed the code that allowed the aliens to hack our satellites and have control of all our systems."

The president tells him he thought Michael was already dead. "No, it's his friend James."

Mr. Parker gives the address to his agents to come and fetch him because he knows that it is already too late to have a solution to the problem of which all mankind is exposed to.

As he tries to contact the aliens, he hears a noise. He pulls out his gun, "Who's there?" I'll fire if you do not show your hands up in the air."

Wanting to open her mouth to let her father know she heard everything, Harry covered Sofi's mouth with his hand and whispers, "Are you crazy, do you wanna kill us? Why don't you get my gun here and shoot us in the head?"

"We have to help James before they take him."

"Do you think that your dad is going to let us take him without a fight? You heard him he wanna be the king of the world, so nothing is going stop him to get what he wants without a fight, including you if it is necessary."

Three government's car honk outside behind the hangar and soldiers, armed very well, get out of the cars.

"What's that?" Waleed whispers.

"Please do yourself a favor, and shut up," said Michael.

Waleed passes his two fingers on his lips and zips it.

"I am here," said Mr. Parker to the soldiers.

At the arrival of the soldiers, they find that James is weak and the agent in charge of taking James to the agency asks why he drugged him.

"I was preliminarily questioning him."

"Did he say anything?"

"No just he created the code by error."

James tries to deny it, but no one believes him since he is nodding off because of the drug. Being in their hiding place, Sofi sees the scene and begins to cry, "He told me I never believed him."

"What?"

"That my father is not the person I believe he is."

They take James and put him in one of their cars that will be escorted to the main headquarters. The president and some secretary of state are about to be evacuated in a secret place where the president can follow the operation.

Michael, Harry, and Waleed try to convince Sofi to give up which Sofi refuses.

"What do you want to do then?" asks Harry.

"I want to follow them."

"No way, we cannot do anything besides going home, and figuring out a plan," said Michael.

Sofi tells them that nothing could stop her from following them, she must know where they are taking him, and that they are not constrain to go with her. Harry looks at Michael and says, "Your buddy is lucky to have a girl like that."

"Yeah I know, I think you'll do the same if you knew him. James deserved to be loved by everyone. For a while, I was jealous of him because he makes Carol laugh in the way I can't," confessed Michael.

"I didn't see her full of life since last year until I saw her in the living room with James one morning," said Harry.

Sofi looks at Harry, and she raps out, "What! Living room! Carol, James, what happened?"

"Oops, I'm out of here," said Michael.

The area becomes too sweaty for Harry, he turns red for a moment but remembers that nothing happened they are just friends.

"Nothing, they stayed up all night talking about you, and slept in the leaving room," he says.

"You see, about me, he was talking about me, that is why I have to go free him from the devil. Sofi believes that she owes him, and it is because of her if he is in that kind of trouble. He knew that going out with me wasn't good for him, but he did just because he loves me," cried Sofi.

"Fine, you are very stubborn girl; nothing can stop you," said Harry.

They take their car and follow James with a considerable distance between their car and the director's escort.

Worried in the bunker, Carol and her mother and neighbors are waiting for her father and her friends with the hope that they bring James with them; she receives Rawan's call. She asks her what's new in Iran because it is seriously bad on her side, she is living the most horrible day of her life and soon she will not be able to bear it anymore. Rawan tells her that she called James's number and she does not get any signal and she is not even being transferred to a voicemail.

"I think James is being held as a prisoner by the government," Carol said.

"Why?" Rawan asked firmly.

"They think James is responsible for the NASA satellite hacking that allowed the aliens to take control of our planet," said Carol.

"And what is your thought?"

"That his computer was trapped," said Carol.

"Here, every moment we breathe is a miracle for my family and I. This is the time when you would not like to be a person who's responsible for a country or a senior government official," said Rawan.

Carol tells Rawan that she is having the same nightmare and that she could not able to bear the loss of Michael, it will kill her before the aliens do.

"Where is he?"

"He's with Waleed and my father and Sofi out looking for James."

"Who is Sofi?"

"You know Sofi, James's girlfriend."

"Ohhh, that Sofi."

After a good moment of thinking, Rawan asks Carol if she is sure the government holds James. Carol confirms it, and Rawan thinks that she might have an idea.

"What?" asked Carol.

Rawan tells her that if it is really James who allowed the aliens to hack the system, he can hack it and take the control again.

"Yes Michael thinks that's why they are holding him."

"What! I don't understand; the president would put him in detention knowing that he could stop the apocalypse! Isn't that crazy!" said Rawan.

Carol reports that it is not the president; she does not know why people in his administration are doing everything for the aliens to succeed.

Rawan explains her idea, which includes telling her father, Hassan, to tell her uncle to speak to the president of the US.

"That's fraternizing with the worst enemies ever. He won't have it." said Carol.

"I have to try. We just have to hope for the best."

Rawan hangs up following the corridor leading to her room, she overhears her father frightened, talking with her mother about what is going to happen if the aliens take control of their country. They will be the first to be killed because they are government officials. Rawan goes into the room without even knocking which is not polite in Iran. Pops in and says, "I know someone who could help us before it's too late."

"The father asks her what she is talking about."

"I'm talking about someone who can make the aliens disappear before it's too late," said Rawan.

"Who?" asked her father.

"That's the problem, it is a citizen of an enemy country."

"Currently an enemy country does not exist, tell me your plan," Hassan said enthusiastically.

Without hesitation, she speaks earnestly to him that he is a friend living in the USA. Hassan is intrigued about the friend, "You have an American friend? How could that be possible?" That's why he did not want her to go to the USA.

"You think this is a good time to talk about it?"

"Right, that can wait, but if we survive you will be deprived of getting out of your room for life."

"Daaaad."

State Minister Hassan treats his daughter of a naïve young girl; saying that if this young man was sure to be able to stop it, he will have done it already.

She must not forget that she is talking about an American who will have shown his arrogance to impress the world if he was able to.

"Dad you're wrong, James is different, no one knows him and he always makes sure his life is secret," said Rawan.

"How do you know that then if nobody knows about his skills?"

Rawan lets her father know that she had promised him not to say anything to anyone, but as he insisted she could tell him why she had confidence in him. She brings up the story about her computer that James has decoded, something that several geeks could not.

"What do you mean? Your mysterious friend has neutralized the virus that the biggest specialist in the country has set up?" said Hassan.

"I knew it, why would you do that?" Rawan whimpered.

"You were going to the USA honey," said Hassan with his Persian-English accent, "by the way, tell me how do you want us to get help from someone who's in the USA?"

"That's where you come in; the US government has him in detention because they think he is responsible for this."

"How do you know that?" asked her father

"I called his friends."

Hassan still does not know how he might be helpful, so he wants to know the part where his help is needed. Rawan stares at her father in the face with a frustrating look.

"No, no, no I am not gonna do that, the president would be brain-dead for that to happen." Said the state minister.

"Why?" she asked.

"Because, because."

"It doesn't mean anything."

"OK because the USA is never going to listen to Iranian's president, they hate us more than North Korea."

She reminds him that he said before there is no enemy at this time, and he does not have anything to lose trying, maybe it would help.

"OK, I will see if your uncle is going to accept, I don't promise."

"What? Will! No, we don't have time, now, call him now," snapped Rawan.

The state minister takes his phone, and calls the president of Iran to ask him a favor that might help them. At the end of the call, Hassan is impressed by the conversation, it was not like he has expected the president to accept his request unthinkingly. He just realized how people declaring war against other countries love life they'll do anything to stay alive.

Chapter 18

James in the White House

Having lost track of the government's vehicles after having a flat tire, they continue on foot looking for a car. On the way, Waleed catches a brief glance of a girl stuck into her upside-down car when everybody is running looking for somewhere to hide in panic. Waleed runs to rescue her.

"Don't worry, I'm here to help you, you can't stay there," he said.

"My bag is stuck behind; you help me unhook it?" asked the girl

After getting her out, he helps her pull out the bag, but the bag is stuck. The car begins to catch fire. "Waleeeeeed, run, the car is on fire," yelled Michael.

She does not want to let go; Waleed lifts her up, carry her by force and runs. The car explodes, some debris reached Waleed on the arm, and he fall, passes out from the shock.

Michael and Sofi come to help him while Harry is looking for a car. They take Waleed and join Harry who finds them an old lemon that hardly moves. Michael asks the girl her name.

"My name is Lexi Ramses," responded the girl.

"OK! Come with us, it is not safe out here. We have a safe place, but we are looking for our friend first before we go home."

"OK, I don't have anywhere else to go," she said.

On their way to the white house, Sofi slaps Waleed to wake him.

Waleed jumps up, "Do you treat people like that in heaven?"

"What?" She asked surprisingly

"What is wrong with you to slap me like that?"

"I thought you were dead."

"You see now I wasn't," he snapped.

"So why did you talk about heaven."

"I don't know, did I say heaven? I think I was dreaming."

She looks at Michael and asks Harry if this is a good sign. Harry tells him to explain his dream.

"It's about a girl I saved, a beautiful girl, and she was asking me not to leave her, and you ruined my life by inter…interrumpting, no, interrupting my dream; I won't see her again."

"Do you feel any pain?" said Sofi with a bizarre face.

"No, why I'm gonna feel pain?"

Sofi asked him to look at his arm, after seeing his injury he starts crying, "Oh, noo. When did this happen?"

"When you saved my life," said Lexi in the back seat.

Waleed raises his head, "It wasn't a dream, how long have you been here, I…I mean in the car."

"Since you saved my life."

"OK! Did you hear what I just said about my dream? Please say no," he muttered.

"Sorry, I heard."

"Wow, this is so embarrassing."

Michael, Sofi, and Harry laugh, and Lexi smiled. "Don't be."

"Really?" asked Waleed, looking at her chest.

"Hey, dude, it's not happening down there, it's happening up here; look at my face when we are talking," said Lexi hovering her hand around her face.

"OK! Then you must put something on it, your shirt is so tight like a second skin."

Lexi scowled and looks at the people on the next seat, and she draws a fake smile on her face.

Michael tells her not to worry he is like that, "Do you know why his nickname is Wallaby? Nothing is going on in his little head."

Waleed takes off his jacket, and he gives it to Lexi. From his move to give her the jacket, he starts feeling the pain, the sweat is flowing all along his face. Michael glimpses by the window, and he sees people destroying cars and some of them running, then at his right, he sees a drug store; he tells Harry to stop the car.

"Waleed needs something to disinfect the wound and for the pain."

Harry stops the car, Michael gets out. After 10 feet of walk, he realizes that he doesn't know what to take he comes back, and asks Harry, "I was wondering if you know something in medicine."

"Nothing buddy; but when you serve a long time in the army, and you had like this injury you know what to take before you find a doctor to amputate your leg."

"Whaaaat?" hearing that Waleed faints.

Harry and Michael grin while Sofi and Lexi are worried.

"Come on guys, you want to kill him," said Sofi.

"He is just sniveling for nothing this is not a big deal, but let me go grab something to wake him up."

Harry goes take the medicine, and he comes back. They hit the road again.

In the White House wishing to make the query and see if James will tell him the truth; The US president demands that James is taken to the solitary confinement room. Sometime later, the president arrives in the room, escorted by the director of the CIA and his close bodyguards. James raises his head and looks at one of the most powerful man in the world and says, "Mr. President before you start asking me questions, I would like you to know that I no longer have anything to say to anyone, and above all, if I were in your place I would look for a safer place to hide because this bunker could not be a problem for them."

The president asks the director, who the young man is.

"It's the kid who hijacked our network and put the whole world in danger, and now we have only two choices. One of the choices is to face these monsters and lose a lot of men, and the second is to go to the bunker to avoid the massacre of the population, it is the government they want," said the director.

"What kind of president would I be fleeing and abandoning the people who trusted and elected me, no I would never do that," said the president.

The president looks at James and James says, "In your place, I would listen to him, you cannot control anything anymore."

The president wonders why he did this, why did he hack the system. Being able to find the right answer, James says to him when he was in high school he hacked NASA to find out if someone was really on the moon or if it was a hoax. NASA did not catch him, so he wanted to see what it's like to be the man who caused the apocalypse. James tells him that if this can reassure him, he expected worse than that, but alas "we don't always get what we want."

"It is brave of you to remain here under my authority without handcuff and say whatever you want, but keep in mind that when they arrive here, you will be their welcome gift." said the president angrily

The president leaves the room with despair, followed by his bodyguards.

Mr. Parker comes near James looking for answers about what he just said, "I told him the truth, it's too late, you win."

"So what were you talking about saying that if I release you, you could avoid that?"

"I was bluffing; I wanted to be free and get out of there to find a shelter like everyone else."

Mr. Parker walks out of the room smiling, knowing that he has reached his goal.

James thinks of his family living in California, and what his cousin, nephew, and sister in law living New York have become because of him, he begins to cry. Alone in the room, he stands up and inspects the room to see if there are hidden cameras.

All of a sudden, the door opens and the president enters the room, his closest guards wanting to follow him, he tells them to wait outside.

"Sir!!!"

"Stay here! It's an order."

The president enters and sits near James and shows him the terror he caused in the world after two-minute of silence, James asks the president why he came alone this time, where is Mr. Parker.

"I wanted to show you your crimes in person; the director has work to do. Wait, how do you know that the director of the CIA is called Parker?"

James beckons the president to say nothing; he approaches his ears and asks if there are any cameras or microphones in the room. The president gets up turns around and comes near James, smacks him and asks what he is trying to do again.

James explains to the president how the hijacking took place and how far the director of the CIA is involved.

"Are you out of your mind? Mr. Parker is the most faithful director I've ever seen in my whole life," said the president.

"I know what I'm talking about because I'm his daughter's boyfriend from high school. Did you ask your Rangers in what condition they found me in the warehouse?"

"I think every agent has his way of doing their interrogations, and Mr. Parker always gets results in his queries."

"OK! Did he tell you that I have an idea how to stop this?"

"What! You just said it's too late."

"Because we were not alone in the room and I hardly trust people especially when it comes to life or death, and unfortunately your director of the CIA is part of the villains."

"And you trust me?"

"I believe that after seeing your face when I said it is too late. I have seen in your eyes how much the population that elected you counted for you, so yes."

"How can you do something that our entire specialist could not?"

"I can try." James does not really trust the president so he keeps the details of how he can stop the disaster for now.

"What tells me you're not going to make things worse?" said the president.

"worst, more than they are already?" smiled James.

"Yes, of course, by giving them access to nuclear weapons."

"What tells you they don't have them?"

Someone knocks at the door and James become silent.

"Mr. President," said someone behind the door.

"Who's that?"

"Someone on the phone for you, and he said it's very important."

The president wanting to leave in a rush tells James to think about what he is saying, James grabs him by the hand and begs him not to talk about what he told him to anyone, even to his entourage. The president leaves, ang goes back to his office, the US president wonders who is trying to reach him at this desperate time.

"This is the Iranian president," said the secretary

The president engages a peaceful conversation then he asks what the call of the Iranian president is about.

After taking the phone from the hands of the secretary the president of Iran asks if the phone is secured. The head of the White House request to his secretary to go.

"Yes, currently all the phone in the White House are secured. What is it?" said the US president.

The Iranian leader explains the reasons of his call, without forgetting to tell him that his government is corrupt according to his source. And no one should know that James is free, if not the only chance that mankind will be spared from this catastrophe will fall.

"I just want to know, how do you know about James?" asked the president.

"James is a friend of a friend, and she believes he could do it."

"OK, do you know who the spy in my government is?"

"I don't know, but he is in a very important post."

"Thanks, mister president. It was very nice talking to you, and for the help that you provided to Saudi Arabia."

"I think we have to help each other to protect our planet, thank you too."

The president returns to the crisis room and orders to the statisticians to evaluate the loss of life and material they will suffer if they decide to confront the aliens. Being confirmed that his government is corrupt, but is still, does not believe that it is the director of the CIA. The President goes to James's cell and tells him that he has just received a call from one of his friends and that he has confirmed what James said to him, but the only difference is that he does not know who the spy is.

"What friend is that? Michael, I knew he would not give up."

"No, it's an Iranian friend, I think according to the Iranian president."

"I don't know any Iranian friend who could contact you directly. Unless, it's a trap."

"So how could she know your name, wait, do you know Michael?"

"Yeah, he is my best friend, he was the first to be arrested by the FBI at the beginning of the chaos."

"I think we have a friend in common."

"Do you know Michael?"

"Yes, he has agreed to be delivered to the aliens for the survival of the planet, after the aliens have asked to see him."

"And what do you think they did to him?" asked James

"I really don't know."

On the road, Waleed wakes up, and he takes the painkiller, "Did you just kill me for a second time?" asked Waleed to Harry.

"No, it's a bad dream dingus," said Sofi.

Arriving at the entrance of the White House, they see protesters and many battle tanks and many soldiers, at 50 feet to the entrance, there are barricades that forbid whoever to pass.

Harry stops the car and Michael gets out of the car with his hands up in the air, "My name is Michael, I want to talk to the president."

"Yes that's it; I would like to know the mystery that hides in the triangle of Bermuda while we are on the impossible wishes," said the command of the security.

"Who is the boss here?" Asked Michael.

"I'm the boss."

"OK! The boss, do you think if it wasn't important I would be here instead of looking for a safe place somewhere far away from here to hide? Tell the president that it is Michael Ponson, and don't forget to tell him that it's the Michael the hostage that was taken by the aliens."

"No way, I heard about it. Tell me how you did to stay alive after seeing those creatures because the FBI agent that saw them for the first time lost his mind."

"It's a long story we don't have time, call him."

The command tries to use his phone to call. Michael pulls out the phone of his hand, and he tells him not to do it the White House is not trustworthy. The command goes inside to tell the president that Michael wants to talk to him, but the secretary doesn't want the commandant to go inside the room. The commandant urges her to let him go, and more she makes him wait, the more she increases the percentage of the people who are dying. She lets him go in the office.

After telling him, the president couldn't believe that Michael is alive until he looks through the window and sees him. He tells him to escort Michael and his friends inside, but by the secure door that is used just for these kinds of circumstances.

Chapter 19
The Reunion

The president goes to the room where James is, and breaks the news for him that his friends are here. James had his head down when the president entered and said friends, he jumps, “Where are they?” he said.

“Come with me, you’ll see by yourself.”

“Do you think it’s a good idea, I mean Mr. Parker is not supposed to know that we have a plan?”

“Mr. Parker is not here, he vanished.” James follows the president. After long way walking in the hallway of the White House, James starts wondering. He thinks that they are going to put him somewhere where nobody is ever going to hear about him again for the rest of his life, but like always, he knows how to be patient.

Once at destination, the president’s secret service agent opens the door. James looks inside the room, he sees his friends. Sofi runs, jumps in his arms, shedding tears of joy.

“What happened?” said Sofi.

James looks at Waleed.

“I didn’t say anything,” said Waleed.

“Can I borrow him for a second?” said Mr. President.

“Yes sure Mr. President,” said Sofi.

The president introduces James to his wife, and his little daughter, and his staff’s family who were in the room since the aliens delivered the message that they are going to take the control of the country. The president asks James what they should do. He says if it is possible he needs the list of the best hackers in the world. The president makes a call to the director of the FBI.

James forgot to look around him, since he saw Sofi.

“Hey buddy how you doing, I heard that you had a little chat with our guests,” said James.

“Yeah, how about you? We were following you until our car stopped.”

"We were at the warehouse when you were having a great time with your father in law, but we couldn't save you."

"Ohhh, did you see the director of the CIA?" asked James.

"Yeah, here at first and then when he held you in captivity. I think he is scarier than the aliens. What do you think?"

"I couldn't tell, I haven't been taken by the aliens."

James looks at Sofi sitting with Waleed silently, lost in her mind, he feels the pain of the torture she going through after witnessing the things that her father did.

"Were you with Sofi there?" He asks James while staring at Sofi.

"Yeah she brought us here, she is really stubborn."

"Can I leave you alone for a moment I want to talk to her."

"Yeah, absolutely."

James joins Sofi, "Hi, little girl how are you?" he smiled.

"Hi, little boy I'm good."

"Do you remember when we first met?" he asked to casually to get her mind out of the depressing thoughts she is having.

"Yep, you toppled me down with my books in my hands."

"If only I could go back in time. I am really sorry sweetheart for everything, all this is my fault I should not have introduced my problems into your life. All this happened because of my selfishness. I'm so sorry," said James while whimpering.

Sofi cannot let him blame himself for all of it, nothing of it is his fault; he has always been there for her, even to protect her against herself.

James is worried about her seeing the true face of her father in the warehouse. He asks her at what time they arrived at the warehouse.

"You want to know if I was in time to hear the conversation you had with my father!"

"No, no."

"I heard it was him who blocked my access to Harvard, and you pirated the system that caused the apocalypse, but I have something that intrigues me."

"What?" asked James.

"Why are you protecting this monster," asked Sofi.

"Just because it's the father of the girl I fell in love with, and I would not want anything that could break her heart."

Waleed is lying in the bed fantasizing about the young Lexi, he can no longer be patient especially when she is sitting next to him. Waleed approaches her upright, and he kisses her, busted by James, he panics, "Ouch! You bit me." said Lexi.

"Sorry, it's not my fault, he scared me," said Waleed.

“Sorry I didn’t know that you were busy here. I’ll come later,” said James.

Lexi tells James to stay, she was leaving anyway to go check her lip.

“Hi man!” asked James.

“Hi! We were thinking that you were going to die once you get here,” said Waleed.

“Yeah me too. I mean I was gonna die, and then the president told me that the president of Iran and I had a friend in common who believes that I’m innocent,” said James.

“Wow, a friend from Iran.”

Waleed knows who the friend is, but pretends not to understand. Michael knocked at the door, then comes in, “They have the list you’ve asked for, and do you think your plan will work?”

“Yes, we must try.”

“OK! By the way, did this Somalian pirate tell you how he got this on his arm?” asked Michael.

Waleed shakes his head vigorously to Michael to say nothing. Too late, James saw him move his head so he asked what happened.

“Yeah, tell him or I will,” said Michael.

“Fine, you are a pain in an ass you know that!” said Waleed.

Waleed explains his awful story to James, and James laughed. Michael and Waleed are confused. “At least you didn’t put your life in danger in vain.” He said

“What?” Asked Michael and Waleed shakes his head to James. “I found them eating each other’s mouth when I came in.” Laughed James. “Come one people. Remind me to never trust you with my secret.” Said Waleed.

“It wasn’t a secret. You got busted. That was stupid though.”

“Yes, I know, but you see, I saved the life of my future ex-girlfriend,” smiled Waleed.

“Stop piffling.” James and Michael make him promise that he will never do it again. His face changes, he tries to hold his tears. They feel awful that they have offended him. “Do care that much about me?”

“We all worry about each other man, you know that.”

With an air of astonishment, Waleed looks at his friends and his tears continue to flow all the way down his cheeks. James asks why he is crying if it’s because of his injury.

“It’s just because I did not know that you care about me like that,” he sobs.

Lexi comes in with a glass of water for Waleed. Michael tells James leave the room

"Yes, now gerrrara here," said Waleed, Lexi smiles and closes the door behind them. Michael returns back grabs the door and says, "Don't do anything stupid; it's not a motel, it's the White House."

"I should be able to say one day, I did this in the White House. Now go away you're so annoying," responded Waleed.

On the way to the main hall of the bunker, Michael asks James if he is OK because he knows that his last hours have not been easy.

"Since last year I have been wondering what kind of parents would abandon their three-year child and go away without ever looking behind, and today I realize that they have never been far, they never had the luck. The most shocking thing is that the person who killed them is the father of the love of my life. So…I'm not OK." said James.

"Now what do you intend to do?"

"About what?" asked James.

"About your father in law." Smiled Michael.

"Stop calling him my father in law, and I think at the moment we have something else to worry about that is more important than personal revenge." he said and gets up.

While the president comes to give the list of hackers in person to James, the NSA analysts are trying to have a solution.

Having noticed the absence of the president at the oval office, Mr. Parker goes into the crisis room and he does not find the president, he heads into the room where James is detained he finds no one. Knowing that James will never be displaced without his knowledge, he realizes that he has been compromised. He empties his office and disappears.

Escorted by two of the agents he formed throughout his command in different positions occupied in the government. Then, he goes to his friends, aliens, to tell them to accelerate the procedure, which is to abandon other countries and to focus their attention on the president of the USA, because the best way to take control of the planet is to fight the strongest. The president of the USA is the one who must be put out.

The leader of the aliens asks Mr. Parker what his plan is, they must be in contact with their army before starting a war otherwise they would risk losing if they are fewer and less armed.

Mr. Parker informs him that after having contacted their soldiers, they should immediately come to the ground and opt for martial law, because humans will not surrender easily. Wishing to leave the spaceship; he turns around, "I forgot to tell you that this day has generated a strong link between the worst enemy of the planet like Russia, the USA, and the North Korea, can you imagine! Tic toc, tic toc the time is running, hurry up." He leaves the UFO followed by his bodyguards.

James asks the president if he can talk to him alone with Michael and Sofi.

"Yeah, follow me to my office," said the president.

They follow him in the Oval Office, James wonders in the Oval Office in circles to see if he can see a camera. After watching him for a while believing that James is admiring the place, the president says to him, "Amazing, right?" with a smile

"What?" asked James.

"The office, you are admiring it for a long time now."

"Yeah it's amazing, but I wasn't admiring it I was looking for cameras."

"Oh OK! Isn't he weird?" whispered the president to Sofi.

"Yes, he is," smiled Sofi and Michael.

"I heard that," said James.

The president tells James that there are no cameras in the office. James pulls up his pants, puts his hand in his sock, and he takes out the flash drive that he had to hide during the beginning of the invasion.

"What is that?" asked the president

He holds the key and shows it to them, "This is the program that we need to defeat their plan."

"What's that?" asked Michael.

"The code," said James.

"How did you get hold of that?"

"I had it copied the same day that you gave me Steve's computer."

Michael moves his head and says "You, little piece of shit. That was genius."

The president asks him what he's talking about. "So why did you ask for a list of hackers?" asked Michael.

James approaches Michael and says, "I asked for this list because considering the duration and the conditions of which the flash drive was in, I think we will need to redo the code and only the two of us won't be able to do it."

"How are we supposed to make a code that we cannot know where to begin?" asked Michael.

"I memorized the essential parts."

Michael grabs his hand and sits on the couch while the president is on the phone and Sofi continues to contemplate the Oval Office.

"How can you memorize that kind of stuff?" whispered Michael to James's ears furiously, "Are you insane, make sure nobody knows about this, even the president, OK, otherwise, you're a dead man. I do not believe my ears that you have memorized the only thing capable of making an apocalypse, what were you thinking," Michael said angrily.

The president does not understand how hackers away from American territory can help. After receiving a long list of names, James reduces and selects the six first hackers of different countries, and asks the president to give it to his intelligence services to locate them. The president asks James to follow him in the crisis room that he has his generals waiting for him.

"Mr. President I think this is not a good idea," said James.

"Do not worry, Mr. Parker has vacated his office long time after knowing that he was uncloaked, he is accompanied by security agents who are faithful to him."

"OK! But I have something to tell you, Mr. President."

The president sits down with a frustrating air believing that James's plan has a strong probability of not working.

James raises his head and looks at Michael, wanting to leave the room, he asks him to stay.

James apologizes for his unfortunate remarks he made about him in the interrogation room because of Mr. Parker's presence. The president smiles, "Is that all?" he Asked

"Yes, that's all."

The president lets out a sigh of relief, "You gave me goose bumps, I thought that our plan wasn't going to work. There is nothing to forgive. You have done well. In fact, I'm the one who owes you an apology for not having believed in you at the beginning, at least before your mysterious friend of Iran speaks to the Iranian president."

Michael ways in into the conversation. He asks James what Iranian friend the President is talking about. James shrugs. Michael looks at the president cannot resist of asking him if James's friend is a girl.

"I don't know, he only said a friend of James, I can call the president and ask him if you want," said the President

"Yeah, absolutely." He shook his head.

"What if it was Rawan?" muttered Michael to James.

"You grew up in a cave or what? We're talking about Iran here; not a country where a little girl talks to a president freely without seeing her head separated to her body." whispered James to Michael.

"Hum, you have a point."

On their way to meet the staff of the president; The president opens the door of the Oval Office and stops a moment after a reflection and says, "James, I would like to know if it is true that you once have hacked the NASA without no-one realizing it, or was it part of your ruse to make Mr. Parker believe it's too late."

"If I admit it, would I be in trouble?"

"No, I don't think so," sneered the president at him.

"Funny," smiled James and he holds the door for the president.

In the situation room, accompanied by James and Michael, the president asks his generals if they have room for few guests.

"It's against the protocol Mr. President," said the Admiral Notch Atarday.

"I don't think there would be any protocol if these boys don't help us. Unless, you have an alternative."

"No we don't, and how can they help us?"

The president explains to his generals and advisers the causes of his repetitive absences from the meeting after receiving the call of the Iranian president.

After a long tergiversation of the commanders, the president takes out the list of hackers and the flash drive, "It is not a request; it is an order that I politely gave, do not abuse of my patience. I'm running out of it."

"Yes, of course, Mr. President," said one of his secretaries.

The president gives them the list to find the exact locations of the hackers.

Having localized the hacker one by one in different places of the globe that are in North Korea, Russia, USA, China, a West African country and Pakistan. They are apprehended and led against their will in American embassies but convinced by their country leaders, they agree to cooperate.

Chapter 20

The Last Hope

After receiving explanations of their presence in the US territories abroad through conference calls, the computer geniuses accepted to help James and Michael to save the world except for the hacker named Bilal. He refuses to help because the government is the one asking.

"Who is this young man?" wondered the president of the United States facing James.

"He is from West Africa, he is called Bilal Almery and had an appalling history with his government that is not in the record," James said after isolating the call line.

The president tells the director of the FBI and the deputy director of the CIA to see what can be found in this man's life. while they try to make him cooperate.

Immediately, his government receives the call of the president of the United States asking about Bilal. The president claims to know nothing about why Bilal has beef against him. The FBI and the CIA present themselves without any record on Bilal and nothing regarding the subject. While Bilal is detained against his will at the US Embassy. His president has a dilemma which is showing his true face or lying to save his reputation. Having nothing to find, the President of the United States call and asked to speak to the young man.

"Hello, this is the president of the United States."

"So…" said Bilal.

The president raises his head bewildered, and looks at the people in the room, and he smiles, *how could he have the nerve to talk like that to the most powerful man in the world,* thinks the president, but he does not dare to say it because he needs his help.

"I want to know why you don't want to help," asked the president.

"Because I'm not the kind of help you need, and you don't deserve my help. You're all the same, now unless you have something against me, I want to go home," said Bilal.

"Can you tell me what is between you and your government?"

"He's the president and I'm the villain," retorted Bilal angrily.

"What are you going to tell your family if the apocalypse begins and people die knowing you could have prevented it?"

"I would tell them that people had what they deserved, and justice is done."

Having heard this, Michael is researching the parents and finds that two years ago, Bilal hacked the government system and he discovered something that he was not supposed to see. He made the mistake of publishing the documents to denounce the corruption of the government, on behalf of the people. And that caused a fatal blow to the government. The retaliation of the government cost the lives of his family. No one had raised a little finger to bring to justice the culprits. Since that time Bilal did not appear on any radar until today.

After having received information on the basis of his refusal to cooperate; Michael puts the file under James's eyes as he tries to convince Bilal. James reads the document and asks the president for permission to isolate the line so that he can speak alone with Bilal.

James isolates the call and tells a little story to him hoping that this makes him feel better, ending with, "I know that you are not selfish and your family was a victim of your government like mine, And I assure you, those times are in the past. At this time, it is not the government that needs your help, it is the whole planet. Today, your government does not have the power, you have the power, now decide what you're going to do with the power you have."

"What are you talking about? You're just a simple citizen; they ask you for help right now, as soon as you become useless to their cause, you become disposable, they won't care about anyone even you; that's how it's works with politicians," Bilal said angrily.

"I promise, you will have the justice you deserve," said another voice in the conference.

"I beg your pardon!" Bilal asked.

"I am your president, I promise that you will have your justice," said the president of the West African country.

Bilal accepts the deal. He puts down the phone. The security agents of the US Embassy give him the equipment he needs.

It's been two years since Bilal had lost the desire to smile. Bilal is paranoid exactly like James, he does not believe a word of what both presidents said, he just agreed because of what James said. As soon as he finishes, he'll vanish again where no one can find him.

Being on the same page now, everyone is in front of his screen and in front of large screens, allowing them to be in visual audio communication, James shows them the code they must program. This code is the only way to prevent the aliens from communicating with their home planet and allowing them to bring their alien armies to annihilate humanity.

"OK, we do not have much time; that's why I didn't want the NSA analysts. I know together we can do what an army of any analyst firm can't do, good luck, the world relies on us." said James.

They start typing on the keyboards.

Each state that is invaded by UFOs, deploy more and more soldiers, knowing that their soldiers are weak in front of these creatures and their weapons they stay vigilant, but the important thing is that they must at least gain time until the code to foil the Machiavellian plan of the aliens to be executed be ready. After hours of hard work, they reach their goal. The code is ready, and the most difficult part is to go into the UFO and plug the flash drive into the central server to insert the virus that could prevent any communication with their planet. The various branches of the US Army, the NSA, CIA, and FBI put all the resources at their disposal in the hands of James and the best soldiers of the army formed for this kind of mission. General Bac Samson charged with the mission demonstrates his strategy that he will adapt to the US president and advisors.

Waleed enters the room without knocking, "Who's this penguin?" asked General Bac.

"It's my friend, what are you doing here? You're not supposed to be there," muttered Michael to Waleed.

Michael stands up and walks Waleed out the room when they arrive at his room, Waleed stops walking, "When you are ready to go, you are going to call me, right?" asked Waleed.

"For what?"

"I'm going with you."

"No, you're not."

"I was sure you'd say that."

"Then don't be disappointed."

"I wanna help."

"You are helping us by staying here with Lexi."

"She can take care of herself," said Waleed.

"I heard that…" shouted Lexi behind the door.

"Sorry…" responded Waleed.

Michael opens the door and tells Lexi to help convince Waleed that he can't go. Lexi reminds Michael that she just met him, what makes him think he'll listen to her.

"You see, she is right!" panted Waleed.

"Shut up dude, you are hurting my feelings," raped out Lexi, "what a clown."

"Say it again." Waleed said

"You are so unromantic, I thought you are going to say of course, she could make me stay," said Lexi.

"I think I heard word feelings."

"I don't know what you are talking about," said Lexi and she runs to the join the others in the living room.

Michael smiles, bend over the door to get out, and Waleed grabs his hand and says, "Be careful out there, and keep eye on James."

"I will."

Waleed goes to join Lexi for a clarification on what he has heard. Michael goes back to the crisis room.

After the briefing, they are ready to face their destiny. James knows that he cannot do anything to stop Sofi from following him to the suicide mission he's about to go to because she feels responsible for all that's going on, but it's worth trying. James calls Sofi and Michael to talk to them privately in another room. In the room, James begins groping; Sofi looks at Michael and asks him what's wrong, Michael ducks his head.

"It's time to go now," said James.

"Yeah I know, so what are we doing here?" asked Sofi, James becomes silent the second time.

"I know what you're going to say, please don't," said Sofi sobbingly, "I'm not staying." She stars crying.

"Please Michael, explain to her," said James.

"Sofi he is right, and you know that. He cannot take the risk to let you come with us."

"No, no, no why? That's unfair, I'm coming." She continues crying.

James approaches her and hugs her tightly against him. Michael goes to wait at the door. Sofi looks up and glances at James with gloomy eyes.

"Your eyes are shinning with all the tears you have held since the first day we met. Ever since I came back into your life, I only brought trouble in it," groaned Sofi.

"Don't say that, since you got back into my life. You enlightened it. I can't bear your absence in my life as I promised you, you'll like it in Boston, and we have all the life in front of us. The only thing I ask is that you stay here and wait for me," pouted James.

"James, it's time they're just waiting for us," said Michael behind the close door.

Sofi stays glued at him, she leans her head on James's chest and does not want to let go.

"Please, wait just one minute," she said.

While standing there, James express the feelings of forever goodbyes.

"I missed you Sofi; I missed your foolishness, your smile, your laugh, and your hands on me. I love you, and I will always love you." Cried James.

"Me too and come back to me safe," said Sofi.

James kisses her on the forehead and leaves the room. Lonesome, Sofi stays in the room for a while sobbing.

General Bac Samson introduces the soldiers who will go on the battlefield to the president of the US, who is being very grateful for their bravery and the sacrifice that they are about to make.

"What are these G.I Joes doing here?" James asked the President when he enters the room and sees the soldiers.

"They will bc with you to ensure your safety," said the President.

"You are James and you are Michael, I suppose. I'm Commandant Alijah, nice to meet you."

The president approached Michael and hugs him for this time before saying goodbye, and tells him that it is the second time he puts his life in danger for the country. "Mr. President, everybody got to do what he got to do, and I am very happy to serve my country," said Michael.

"OK then are you ready?"

"Yeah, just two last calls."

"Take your time."

Michael calls Carol to explain to her the mission, which she encourages because she has no choice. The second call to his family, thanking them for all they have done for him and that he loves them strongly. Michael doesn't tell them what he is about to do.

Jamcs joins the president, standing impressed by the sacrifice of young generation for the future generation. "It has been an honor for me to meet you, Mr. President," said James.

"The honor is all mine, James...you taught me a lot of things."

James reaches out to the president hand for a farewell greeting; the president declines his hand and takes him in his arms embraces him, "Come here son, promise me to do your best to come back in one piece because we have not yet made acquaintance, and you did not tell me about the NASA thing in high school," the president laughed.

"I promise Mr. President; I know it's too much but I have a favor to ask you," said James.

"What?"

"I would like you not to leave Sofi alone, otherwise she will follow me, and this could put us in danger or at worse make the mission fail, above all if something happens to her I would never forgive myself. You have to know that when I say watching Sofi it means controlling all her movement, controlling her breathing."

"But, but…"

"I'm just kidding, it's just a way to say Sofi is very stubborn, and you know that she is the daughter of one of your best agents."

"OK, tell me how am I going to do that?"

"I don't know, but I'm sure you'll figure it out," said James and he returned to call his dad to tell him his mission, which they disapprove. They know it's a good cause, but it is also dangerous for a young man like him. "Anyway I've already made my decision," said James to them.

On their way, Harry pops out from the living room, "Where do you think you are going without me?"

"Oh, Mr. Harry you should stay here keep an eye in Sofi, please," said Michael.

Harry accepts the request, and the others leave.

After a frightening stressful ride, they arrive at the place where the UFO is, the soldiers ask James and Michael to wait outside until they inspect the interior.

It is in these kind of circumstances that you have the chance to see people who have never been close to their creator do everything to be close to him. The whole world crosses their fingers so that the mission is realized successfully, the religious pray each one of his side no matter what religion you are in, your prayers are needed.

After inspecting the surroundings, they see the door of the gigantic vault open automatically. Without a second thought, commandant Alijah tells his soldiers to go inside. Michael tries to dissuade them, but in video links with General Bac tells them to follow the orders of their commander. James wanting to follow them is forbidden to do it by Alijah, "Where are you going buddy?"

"We have to go, and get over it," said James.

"Are you insane?"

"Why?"

"Do I have to tell you that you are our last chance to sabotage their plans?"

"So?"

"So you have to wait here until we tell you to go inside."

James retreats while Alijah and his men are heading to the UFO; to their surprise they find no one. They bring James and Michael in. The UFO is a big metallic building that Michael wonders how an engine so big can fly at the speed of light.

Being familiar with the inside of the UFO; Michael leads James in the main control room with few soldiers while the others split up in two groups to visit the premises.

A few moments after being inside, in the corridor leading into the control room, they hear gunshots sounding and an explosion James and Michael run along the corridor and manage to have a place to hide.

Sitting in her corner in the crisis room, Sofi withdraws from the crisis room without anyone noticing it except Harry who follows her and catches her. She asks Harry if it was a way to keep her out of the screen that the president had allowed her to go stay in the Oval Office without any guard.

"Of course not," said Harry.

"You know you are a bad liar."

"No, I'm not!" rapped out Harry.

"OK, I have to go find James he is in danger."

"I knew you are stubborn, but I didn't know you are stupid. What exactly are you gonna do there?"

"Please help me."

"How? Even if we want to, we can't."

"That is why we have to go before the president notices my absence."

Harry and Sofi leave the White House without being caught.

The shots constantly go on and get closer to James and Michael. All of a sudden, a dead silence reigns in the UFO. James asks Michael where to find the control room. Michael shows it to him and unfortunately, they are far away, they will not be able to get there. The aliens know that they are there, it is a trap. James gives the flash drive to Michael and gives him instructions to follow.

"What are you doing?" asked Michael.

"I want to make a diversion and save you time to continue the mission."

"No, we'll go together."

"No, this is not the time for a debate, if I was the one who knew where to find the control room, you would've been distraction for them, so suck it up and go there plug the flash drive when I leave. After connecting the key it will give you 5 minutes to have control of their system and you'd be able to modify everything."

James gets up and heads toward the aliens yelling, "I'm here, don't pull the trigger."

Standing in front of them, he finds all the soldiers dead except Alijah who is seriously hurt crawling on the ground and cannot express himself. James comes slowly to him while the aliens have their guns pointed at him. James takes advantage of this opportunity to make a scandal, "I told, I told you that we're going to die here," he cried and bowed to Alijah and whispered him to the ear, "I'm sorry." The alien approaches him and say to him to get up and he stand up, faced the opposite direction of Michael.

Wanting to get out from his hiding place while James is doing his scene; He hears a human voice coughing in a dark cell, "Who is there? You hear me who is this?" whispered Michael twice.

No one answers. Continuing his way, the human voice restarts, "We are here."

Michael comes and looks through the door where the voice comes from and presses a button that he sees near the door. The door opens, he realizes that they are humans prisoners.

"How many of you are here?" asked Michael.

"Just the 2 of us I think," mumbled one of them in his beard.

As he approaches them, he beholds two faces, enclosed by enormous beards.

"Who are you, and why are you here and how long have you been here?" Whispered Michael

"I am a professor, and this is my friend. What day are we?"

"Today is February 25, 2020."

"We've been here for 12 years. You, what are you doing here?" Mumbled the old man

"We are here to stop the apocalypse."

"It's too late, nobody can stop what is about to happen. This is the last day of humans on Earth."

"What are you talking about?"

"They are smarter than us, they are going to bring their soldiers to eradicate the human race on Earth like the black death and after that bring their population."

"How do you know that?"

"I've helped them."

"Who are you?" swooped Michael.

"My name is professor Layoun," said the old guy.

Knowing that it was not by the will of Professor Layoun for helping them, Michael tries to convince him that there is an idea to defeat the alien. The professor does not want to hear anything. Michael takes out the flash drive and shows it to professor Layoun.

"What's this?" asked the professor.

My friend gives it to me before giving himself to these monsters to save me time. I have to plug and take control of their system.

"And this friend of yours, you think he'll succeed in keeping them occupied?" asked the professor.

"Yes I believe, but I don't have much time, do you want to follow me or not?"

"Yes, good, but Mr. Parker needs help, he will not be able to stand up."

"What did you say, Mr. Parker, that name remind me of a traitor of the nation," said Michael, but when he sees him he does not look like the same because of his beard.

"Traitor of the nation, what are you talking about, and tell me little boy, how did you put yourself in this mess?"

"It's a long story and we have no time for chat at this moment I'm afraid. If my best friend should be decapitated it shouldn't be in vain," said Michael.

Michael helps the professor pick up Mr. Parker and they go into the control room.

Chapter 21

The Compromise

Being in captivity James asks his kidnappers why they do this, and no one answers. The leader of the aliens appears and looks at James, "You look exactly like him, like two drops of water always ready to save the world," said the alien with a soft and slow voice.

Something that he did not expect just happened; he is hypnotized to see an alien speak his language.

"Who are you talking about and who are you?" said James surprisingly.

"Call me Mr. Lee, it is the name I choose to have on your planet, but on my planet, I'm called Jaliyah, second rank soldier of the army in charge of the highest important mission for my people. Unfortunately for you, I think I'll keep the name Lee for quite a while as I planned to stay on planet Earth, maybe forever." Said the alien

"Which planet do you come from and how did you learn to speak our language?"

"Our planet is close to yours called Sapity, but it is invisible to your satellites, thanks to God and to our advanced technology, unlikely us who see all that happens on your planet. We have been observing you for thousands of years from generation to generation. After observing everything created before mankind on Earth. Since you came, we started to see things that we didn't see before, wars, slaughters, and hatred between you, every time that a new generation is born we hope that it will be different, and we are always wrong, we always end up disappointed. Every new generation is worse than the previous one." Continued Mr. Lee

"Everybody, even the kids know how many planets are in the universe I've never heard about this one," said James.

Walking around, he explains and shows James how advanced they are, "You know, it is like when you study physiques and Math. You always hear about imaginary line and real line," Jaliyah take a marker and draws a dotted line behind a diagram that he calls the imaginary line and a continuous line in the diagram that he calls the real line. “I bet you’ve already seen this kind of sketch in your classes, right?”

“Yeah, of course,” replies James abruptly.

“OK, think of the world like that. It’s like a mirror.”

“Why are you here?” asked James.

“I told you it is because of your behavior on this planet.”

“Is that the cause of your presence here?”

“No exactly, our planet is dying because of you.”

“So, you decided to invade ours?” said James sadly.

“Yes, we can say that you are the cause of the destruction of our planet. We wanted to be generous in accepting cohabitation with you, but what idiocy made us believe that would be possible, you don’t love yourselves. Even animals of different species can stand each other. Humans, you are unbelievable, you kill for fame or for military decoration even without knowing the reason of the war, the strongest always attacks the weakest, First World War, Second World War, you create weapons of mass destruction to kill humans like you. Everyone wants to be the strongest. The richest does not care about the poorest; he only thinks about how to raise the maximum amount of money and how to own as many properties as possible, even if it’s to the detriment of the poorest. After long observations, we found that you do not deserve to live on this beautiful planet that you do all you can to destroy. Greed and power have poisoned your souls. You don’t care about nature. Your consumptions of resources are what we qualify as squandering and that became unconceivable to mother nature. She’s tired and giving up which is causing climate change, unpredictable fires, unexplainable death of animals, the birth of new deadly viruses. Even you, the most decent person knew what would happen if you use the code, but you did it anyway. You know why? Because you’re selfish it’s in your blood now.”

After this speech of Jaliyah, James remains convinced that humans deserve a second chance and that he will do everything possible to obtain it.

James seeks to know how humans have contributed to the destruction of their planet. Jaliyah lights the main screen of the UFO and shows James a documentary showing the planet of Jaliyah where people are in the process of extinction caused by the experiments of nuclear bomb launchers every time in the atmosphere or the missions on another planet of the universe to see if they can find somewhere to live after they finishing destroying the Earth. James was delighted to finally be able to turn the attention of Jaliyah so that Michael could finish the mission, but after seeing the video that is terrifying he feels guilty.

“How long does your planet have to live?” he asked.

“It is no longer important. You’ve wasted all your chances.”

"Maybe there will be another solution. I only need to know how many years your planet has."

"Two millinery maximum according to our last observation."

"What? Are you kidding me? This is ridiculous two thousand years, you have all that time; I do not think all evil humans are going to live until the first thousand years. We are going to change."

"You are not going to tell me a thing that I did not expect before from humans and never saw. Do not waste your time. How old you think I am?"

"Maybe forty!"

Jaliyah smiles and says, "I am 377 years old. I am here for a mission if I don't accomplish it what would I tell my people, and if I die which is not about to arrive so soon in any case, not before the first millenary anyways. What will become my people if you don't change? The more you continue your activities the more, we suffer the consequences."

Jaliyah stands up and tells James to follow him. While walking, he remembers that Jaliyah said before he looks like someone. He asks whom he was talking about.

"I thought you forgot about that. You look like your father."

"You know my father?"

"Yes, he and Mr. Parker have been of great help to us."

"Yes, I know Mr. Parker got brainwashed by you, and then he killed my father."

"What are you talking about? I have Mr. Parker and your father here in this UFO."

"My father died years ago."

"Yes, that's what I wanted you to believe. Wait! I'll explain it to you."

James follows Jaliyah, who is heading towards the direction where Michael found them. James hopes that Michael could hear their voices and hide.

Jaliyah continues his explanation, "Your father prevented us from hijacking your satellites to pass through your atmosphere without being noticed 18 years ago, but one of our UFOs managed to pass and escape the radars. Your father went to see the government they didn't believe his story, they tried to silence him not to sow panic. They have delegated the Director of the CIA Mr. Parker to do the dirty job. When Mr. Parker came to Professor Layoun, he was convinced by your father's theory and had to make him disappear as he has been told, but in his way that is to take him out of the country with your mother. Mr. Parker visited them regularly. Being on the run for years with your mother, your father did not know that the government was not the only one trying to track them down. We intercepted them first while Mr. Parker was visiting. We never got your mother."

Arriving in the room where the aliens detained the Professor and Mr. Parker, James swallows heavily, frightened he can't believe that his father is alive; they open the door; no one is inside the room. Jaliyah looks at James with a crumpled face and a look of anger, "Where are they? What did you do?" peered Jaliyah.

He calls his guards to excavate the UFO. He takes James's hand and puts him into the cell and closes, "I knew I should have never trusted you, let's say I was about to give you this last chance you've asked," gazed Jaliyah to James.

After a long search, the guards find Michael and his two companions under a table behind the control room.

Busted, Michael gets out, and says, "Do not shoot please," as he puts his hands up in the air, and he suggests to the others the same unless they want to be massacred by these savages. Apprehended, Michael leaves the flash drive plugged on the server and goes out. The alien guards lead them to their chief Jaliyah; who tells them to go look for James in the other cell.

"Who is James? Your idiot friend, who threw himself into the mouth of the wolf so that you could complete your suicide mission?" asked Professor Layoun.

"Yes."

James arrives and sees three people kneeling in front of Jaliyah. He moves slowly, "Michael! Are you OK?"

Michael turns his head, "Yes I'm fine."

James approaches and looks attentively at the professor and Mr. Parker, he hardly recognizes the director of the CIA because of the beard that hides his face.

"Do you know them?" Michael asked surprisingly.

"Michael, it's him, he is alive," moaned James and starts shedding tears.

"Who are you talking about?" Michael throws a glance at James.

"He's my father and this is the director of the CIA, the father of Sofi."

"What, the Satan who has tortured us these last 24 hours!" asked Michael angrily.

James looks at Jaliyah and asks him how it can be possible while he is approaching, "It's not even 2 hours since I've seen the director of the CIA without a beard and he is healthy."

Professor Layoun stands up from his knees and hugs James, "Oh my son." He tries to hold tears of joy seeing his son since almost two decades, but he cannot.

"Where is Mom? He told me you were not together when they captured you," asked James.

Professor Layoun remains mute for a long time and he shakes his head, "Your mother could not go all the way to the end, she was tired of running. I am really sorry," flickered the professor.

"What do you mean, Dad?" asked James.

Jaliyah is annoyed seeing James and his father crying like kids he decides to react, "You two are so pathetic." He asks two guards to make Mr. Parker and Professor Layoun benefit a bath and shave their beards.

He asks the other two to join him in the main room.

"You invite us into your main room so we can see the massacre that you are about to start," asked Michael.

"That wasn't nice! You think we're monsters. It is for your good that we are doing all of this, believe me."

"Whether you do it for our good or not, you remain monsters."

"I will really get angry if you do not stop confounding us, you are the monsters. Tell me, haven't you been detained here with Sofi? Have you been mistreated? Has anyone harmed you or prevented you from circulating in the building? And above all when you wanted to leave, did you not find the door open? Have you been followed?" shouted Jaliyah angrily.

Michael lowers his head knowing that Jaliyah is right.

"Now let me tell you what the real monsters will do. They will start by finding reasons to hate, such as basing their hatred on a religion or a race. Launch bombs on the most innocent people as possible without thinking about the children and the babies that will be dug up under buildings. No, wait I have a better example, how about those governments that are Clinging to their throne, looting their homeland resources and transferring the wealth outside of the country which allow them to remain on the throne for life while the population is dying of starvation every day. I think I am the only one able to judge anyone in this room."

At the moment they are in discussion; Sofi and Harry are behind the UFO hearing them talk, they wonder how to get into the UFO without being seen or how they can neutralize these unkillable creatures. The Professor and the CIA director come back recognizable in the room.

"Did you finish brainwashing the kids to make you understand who the real monsters are?" said Professor Layoun.

"No, Father, this is not a brainwashing. All that he has said is true. Can you imagine 15 years ago you went to the government to talk to them about your discovery and that made you make hard decision which is to abandon me and run for 15 years, and all of that just to protect their backs," said James.

Michael looks at him anxiously, believing that he is on the aliens' side.

"You, don't look at me like that, you know I'm right," said James.

"Fair enough, let's get to it now," said Jaliyah.

He approaches the main computer to begin the apocalypse. Touching the keyboard, he finds that something is wrong with the computer, the main computer is lagging he calls his engineers to check the problem, and they realize that the system is infected by a virus that has erased the data programs that was able to make them in liaisons with their home planet. After hearing this, he becomes furious, and look directly to Michael asking him with an air of disbelief what he was doing in the control room. Michael, so terrified of what's going to happen, cannot open his mouth to speak, he is petrified. The guards return from the control room with a flash drive.

"What's that?" asked Jaliyah, "You think this will be enough to stop us, you need to have a better idea." He goes to the control room desperately with his guards looking for another idea while the humans are truss up unattended.

Sofi and Harry go into the UFO believing that their friends are in danger. At their first look inside Sofi raises her head, and she sees more than two humans sitting together. Suddenly, she sees the CIA director, she pops out from her hiding place with Harry's gun in her hand she shoots Mr. Parker without thinking back, and the others lay down. James raises his head slowly, "No, do not shoot," he said.

"Why are you still protecting this Moloch after all he has done," said Sofi sobbingly.

James begs her to leave because the aliens probably heard the shot. He tells Harry to get her out by force if necessary, and he urges him to prevent the president from doing anything. No more military operations, all is under control, which Harry does immediately.

Laid down, Mr. Parker is bathing in his own blood. He is shot in the abdomen and he needs care.

"Jaliyah, Jaliyah, please help," cried James.

The aliens come running, "Help him; he needs care, someone shot him," said James.

Not being interested in the death of an Earthling; the aliens turn their back on James. Jaliyah sees James's sad face and feels his pain. "You see how painful it is to see people you love suffer without being able to do anything to help them?" said Jaliyah, "What do you think is going to happen to my people in 1000 years if I do not find them a shelter."

"You're talking about a millennium!"

"Yes, that's the point, you're destroying the planet don't bring us back on the same subject. If we let you on this planet 50 more years, you will make it uninhabitable."

"Please help him, please. You're doing everything to convince us that you're not monsters, prove it to me," said James.

"And what will I have in return since you prevented my mission from happening."

"I'd do whatever you want if you leave our planet for 1000 years."

"Wait! Do I look stupid? You ask me two requests while you negotiate and you are the only one who benefits from my services?"

James gets up on his knees to bow down to Jaliyah. Suddenly, his eyes fall on a recent photo of him on the floor near his father. The Professor picks up the picture and puts it back in his pocket.

"What's that?"

"It's nothing," said his father.

"OK, he is dying what do you have for me?" said Jaliyah.

"Whatever you want, but Earth," replied James.

"OK, take him to the emergency room while I think of something." said Jaliyah to his guards.

Jaliyah detached the other three, and he asks the Professor and Michael to leave the UFO.

"What about James?" asked the professor.

"I have something to tell him."

"I am not leaving without my son."

"Yes, you are; unless you want to see him dead before I kill you or my brother kills you," said Jaliyah, "there he is. Let me introduce you my brother, Adam Shai, as you know him under the mask of director Parker, and I bet you qualify him as Abaddon or master Satan himself, but let me tell you that he was doing his job, he is a nice creature like you call us."

James turns around and sees the brother of Jaliyah, which is none but Mr. Parker's copy. He cannot believe it.

"Yeah, I know I can explain," said Jaliyah.

Mr. Parker's doppelganger waves his hand to them while entering the room, "Hi Mike, hi James, d'you miss me?" he said and passed through.

Michael backs away and says to Professor Layoun, "I think we should go, James will join us when he can all right!"

James tells his father that everything is going to be OK. The professor follows Michael.

"Where were we? OK, to cut it short, some of us can talk your language fluently, and they can take any appearance they want, we can be shapeshifters." said Jaliyah.

His brother returns to the common room with the appearance of James. "You see?" said Jaliyah's brother.

"So, we have people everywhere in the world in all the most powerful governments in the world. You sabotaged our plan here, but it's not too bad, we are more powerful now than before that is why I am going to accept your request. Just remember, you can't change your people to be good people, it's in your DNA. You are always going to hate each other. Remember we've got our eyes on you and on Earth. We are not going to let you destroy it, good luck."

"OK! What should I do?" asked James.

"Nothing, just try to change humans' thoughts, and show them why we were here." Jaliyah gives him back his flash drive. James asks him how people will understand if he is saying the truth. He must have the video of their planet to be able to convince his people what is going on in the other side.

"No never, don't even think about it, you'll have a solution like you always do. You think if you knew where our planet is, you wouldn't have invaded it? Humans take everything," said Jaliyah's brother.

"Yes, you are right."

"Now go ahead, drive Mr. Parker to the hospital for his daughter to finish him up."

"What? How do you know it was her?"

"Yeah, we're watching everything. We have eyes everywhere. This is, daddy has an eye on the sky watching everything."

James reaches out to Jaliyah, who tightened his hand and says, "Don't disappoint me."

Mr. Parker's copy reaches out to James who refuses, "OK! Brother he doesn't want to shake my hand."

"I prefer to stay out of it," said Jaliyah.

"OK! Fine."

Jaliyah contacts all the UFOs on Earth and orders them to release the soldiers that they've captured and take off without delay.

James takes Mr. Parker out of the UFO, and wait for the UFO to take off. James has spent the harshest 24 hours of his life, but doesn't hesitate for a second to wave his hand to Jaliyah in the UFO to wish him a good journey. James leads Mr. Parker to the nearest hospital.

In the hospital, he sees on the TV all the channels showing the departure of all the UFOs throughout the planet. The traffic jam in the streets, people manifesting their joy knowing the world will emerge for a prosperous tomorrow. James knows that this is only the beginning.

He calls the White House to find out if Sofi is doing well. The president takes the call in person, and congratulates him before giving the phone to Sofi. James begins by explaining to Sofi that his father is innocent and that it is a long story, and he is in the hospital with Mr. Parker. They're pulling the bullet out.

"Waleed wants to talk to you, it's about someone pretending to be your friend, I'm giving him the phone."

"Hi, bro you made it, I am proud of you honey."

"Thanks."

"OK! The one who talked about you to the Iranian president is Rawan, his niece."

"What are you talking about? Are you drunk?"

"No, it's her, I knew it before, but I did not want to tell you."

"How did you know?"

"She is the daughter of the prime minister of Iran."

"Wow, thanks, see you soon because we need to talk before I murder you."

Waleed passes the phone to Sofi and goes into Lexi's arms, "Now, tell me do you have feelings for me?"

"I have to think about it," she smiled. Sofi tells James she's on her way to the hospital with the president's secret service.

"I'll be waiting for you."

In the UFO, Adam Shai looks at Jaliyah and says, "We did well, and I wish they would listen to the boy, but I don't count on it."

"Yeah, I hope so we will take care of him, maybe he will change them, he is different, he is full of love, he did this just because of love," said Jaliyah with a soft and slow voice.

Once at the hospital, Sofi doesn't see James; she looks for him everywhere, no trace of him. She goes to her father's room and finds him asleep. She asks the doctor no one saw James. She goes into the toilet and sees two security agents from the hospital on the floor dead. She sees traces of blood that she follows until losing them in the parking lot.

"James has disappeared, Mr. President." Sofi wept bitterly on the phone.